THIS SIDE OF PARADISE

Praise for **This Side of Paradise**

"Layne's tale is a heady mix of conspiracies, alternate identities, and sinister underground laboratories with a creepy schizophrenic villain that readers will love to hate. Recommend this title to thriller fans who will enjoy the ride."

—VOYA

"[Layne] exposes the deficits of a Utopian society with a unique and alarming twist that adolescent readers will particularly enjoy. Engaging characters, witty humor, and page-turning plot make for an exciting read."

—ALAN Review

"A gripping tale."

—Lebanon (MO) Daily Record

"Deserves to be on the giant list of classic young adult novels."

—LYRE Review

"The novel's first-person perspective and cliffhanger ending, mixed in with a little romance and lots of humor, is ideal for the young adult reader."

—St. Charles (IL) Republican

THIS SIDE OF
PARADISE

by Steven L. Layne

PELICAN PUBLISHING COMPANY
GRETNA 2014

First printing, 2001
First Pelican printing, 2002
Second Pelican printing, 2003
Third Pelican printing, 2004
First paperback edition, 2005
First Italian edition, 2005
Second paperback printing, 2007
Third paperback printing, 2008
Fourth paperback printing, 2010
Fifth paperback printing, 2014

*The word "Pelican" and the depiction of a pelican are trademarks
of Pelican Publishing Company, Inc., and are registered in the
U.S. Patent and Trademark Office.*

Library of Congress Cataloging-in-Publication Data
Layne, Steven L.
    This side of Paradise / by Steven L. Layne.
    p. cm.
    ISBN 9781589802544 (pbk.)
    Summary: After his father begins working for the
mysterious Eden Corporation, Jack uncovers a sinister
plot that threatens the existence of his entire family.
    1. Cloning—Juvenile fiction. 2. Utopias—Juvenile fiction.
3. Perfection—Juvenile fiction. 4. Utopias—Fiction.
5. Perfection—Fiction. 6. Cloning—Fiction.
7. Science fiction. I. Title.
PZ7.L44675Thi2001
[Fic]
                                    2001118104

Printed in the United States of America
Published by Pelican Publishing Company, Inc.
1000 Burmaster Street, Gretna, Louisiana 70053

To Valerie Cawley, who comprehends the multiple meanings of friendship . . . and puts them into practice so very well.

And

To Charlie Hilding, Todd McInerney, and Danny Sarelas, the faithful trio who showed up with their lunch sacks and stayed for the end.

Author's Note

The primary purpose of this author's note is to reward my students. As my colleague, Val Cawley, and I have shared this story with our students, it has been a magical experience to witness their genuine responses to the plot and to listen to their mature commentary regarding the theme. Their faith in and enthusiasm about my writing is what keeps me going.

My heartfelt appreciation to the following friends whose encouragement and assistance have strengthened this book: Karen Biggs, Michelle Budt, Kathy Bruni, Val & Don Cawley, Jill Cole, Mary Ann Cook, Kathy Dickson, Dave Grayson, Donna & Meredith Hattendorf, Marilyn Jancewicz, Dave & Joy Towner, Susan Wilke, and Beth Zika.

Major thanks to Ryan McNamara and Nate Baron. The countless hours spent on the jacket design paid off. It's one of the best!

To my family – who have all read the manuscript and been so supportive – I love you! Mom, thanks for continuing the tradition of demonstrating your faith so tangibly. Special love to Debbie and Grayson who allow me my needed time in "the cave." Thanks most of all to God in heaven, who has been so very good to me.

Chapter One

I'm not sure if I can point to one single event that led to my father's decision to move us to Paradise. Maybe it was my mother's drinking – which had been on the increase lately. My father insisted that she drank in order to "cope" with my younger brother, Troy, but I didn't agree. *He* was the one who couldn't deal with Troy; he just wouldn't admit it. Before we discovered the truth about my father, I thought the move was his way of trying to save Troy from his "destructive tendencies." Of course, later on I found out differently.

My grandma Katy, a spry and sassy seventy-two-year-old known to us as "Gram," is fond of saying that my younger brother has "a bit of the devil in him." Actually, Troy is very intelligent; he just uses his intelligence in the wrong way. He challenges the system – school, sports, home, life. He can't accept the way things are to the degree that the average person can, and this puts him in conflict with most adults. He questions everything and *everyone*. Mom used to say he came out of the womb and immediately requested a copy of the doctor's credentials.

Whatever the case, my brother's school suspensions for "failure to show proper respect to authority figures" were paralleling my mother's trips to the liquor cabinet –

which were a source of great concern for all of us. My father was also becoming increasingly frustrated by the fact that no form of reprimand had any effect on my brother.

Gram insisted the move was Dad's way of showing Troy who was boss. "You know how your father likes to control things – he always has," she explained as we neared the house during the last leg of our morning run. Gram's gearing up for another marathon. Says she wants to put more distance between herself and all the old people this time. "Oh, what a time he gave me growing up." There was a trace of nostalgia and something else I couldn't quite identify in her voice. "Troy could grow up to be just like him – except for one thing."

"What's that?" I asked curiously. I was fascinated by my grandmother's keen observations. She knew people, *really* knew them, within minutes of meeting them, and as far back as I could recall, she was never wrong. I remember when some of my father's business associates and their wives came to dinner several years back. Even though we were very young, Troy and I had been allowed to eat at the table. In fact, my father had insisted on it, and he had mother buy us matching suits. As the last car pulled away that evening, he had turned to us all and grinned, "Now *this* was a *perfect* evening. You all behaved wonderfully." I remember him patting Gram's hand as if she were a child and saying, "Mother, I noticed you refrained from telling any of your outrageous stories this evening. It was most appreciated. It could have been a very embarrassing situation for me if you had said something to offend my guests. They are very important people."

"I'm glad I met with your approval, Chip." She looked straight into his eyes, and I saw anger burning there that came out in a clipped, sarcastic response. "Perhaps you'll give me a biscuit as well as a pat on the head." Abruptly, she withdrew her hand from his grasp and started up the staircase. She had gone no more than halfway up when she stopped suddenly, turned to look down at him with eyes that I knew, even then, held the wisdom of the ages, and said quite matter-of-factly, "Your friend, Mitch, the one who tells dirty jokes in front of your children and wears that expensive watch you're so impressed with – he's cheating on his wife." And with that she gracefully ascended the staircase. A month later Mitch's wife left him, and a month after that he was remarried to a woman Gram said had probably just made the varsity pom pon squad at Central High.

"Troy's got heart; he feels things deeply," she told me as we crunched through some autumn leaves on the way to the back porch door. "Your father doesn't. At least not in the way I'm talking about. It hurts me to say it, but my son has always wanted to look the best, be the best, and have the best . . . and he made it clear from the time he was a teenager that he'd do whatever was necessary to get there. No matter who it hurt." I heard the catch in her voice and watched helplessly as a tear made its way gently down her wrinkled cheek. "Your brother wouldn't hurt anyone purposely, Jack." She took my hand, placed it between hers, and rubbed it affectionately. "It's not really that he's rebellious; it's natural for him to question things. Most people just don't understand that. Your father, for example, thinks that moving away from Davenport and enrolling Troy in a private school will change him. But your brother can't be duped into behaving like the typical corporate giant's son. It isn't in his nature. It isn't in yours either," she said winking at me. "You just play the game a little better."

A second theory I had about the move was that my father was trying to please his new boss. The corporation my father had worked for since before I was born was downsizing, and he jumped ship about a year ago. He quickly found a position with a new company called *Eden* which he said offered him tremendous room for advancement. He had been with Eden a little more than two weeks when he christened it the *perfect* place to work. He talked nonstop about Eden's philosophies of business and family. In fact, he told us, Eden was a family in and of itself. I'll admit I thought that sounded a little strange at the time. Looking back, I should have paid more attention to just how strange it was.

As my father explained it, Mr. Eden – the owner and chief executive officer of the company – had purchased all of the land in the tiny village of Paradise which was located about forty miles from our town of Davenport. Interestingly, Mr. Eden sold the homes in Paradise to his employees at a tremendous savings provided they sign an agreement that, should they move, the homes would be resold to him at the fair market price. "And this is the most exciting thing," my father told us at yet another evening meal during which we had, once again, heard far more than we cared to about Eden. "Mr. Eden himself came to see me today, and he's offered us one of the finest homes in Paradise at an incredible price!"

"What?" My mother, who rarely interrupted my father's worship sessions regarding Eden, was genuinely surprised. "Chip, you can't seriously think of moving! The boys have their friends and school. Katy does her volunteer work for the Red Cross, and I have my obligations with the town council. It's not that far of a drive; surely you could . . ." My mother stopped in mid-sentence when she saw the look on my father's face. It was a look that we had seen more frequently since he had begun working for Eden. It seemed, to me anyway, that it was a look of dissatisfaction – not so much with our behaviors as with our *selves*. My father had never been easily pleased, had always held everyone to the highest of his personal standards, but something had changed since Mr. Eden had entered the picture. Now, it appeared, with frightening regularity, we didn't seem . . . *acceptable* to him anymore.

"Susan," he said icily, "I would like to share some good news with this family, and if you would do me the courtesy of trying not to squelch it, I would be eternally grateful." Ever since he went to work for Eden, my father had been very harsh with my mother. His comments were often curt. He spoke down to her, ridiculed her. She began drinking, *I* think, to cope with him, not Troy.

A shift in focus became evident as my father turned his gaze toward Troy and me. "Boys, Eden has a private school for the children of the employees. It is funded and operated solely by Mr. Eden. It has everything the local high school here has and more. Technologically it is superior to any school in the country – quite likely to any school in the world, and you have both been offered the opportunity to enroll tuition free. The only condition is that we move to Paradise. Mr. Eden requires all children who attend his school to be residents of the village."

I could tell two things were going to happen immediately. Troy was going to speak, and Dad was going to lose it. So, I decided to become the sacrificial lamb – a role I was ill-suited to play as I instantaneously developed a serious case of "dry-mouth" at the mere thought of what I was about to do.

"Dad," I ventured carefully into the uncharted waters of rebellion. "I'd rather stay here. I mean that other school sounds great and all, but I'm a junior now, and I'd really like to graduate with my friends. I know it would be an imposition on you, but do you think you could keep driving to Eden, since it's such a great place to work, and we could just stay here?" There. That didn't sound so rebellious. I gave myself an A+ on delivery – until I looked at my father's face. A nasty storm was brewing and just as it was about to begin, Troy drew the attack in his direction.

"What's with this Eden guy, anyway? Why does he want all of his employees' families living in the town where his company is? Why does he want all of their kids in his school? If you ask me, it's bizarre! Why would the boss want his employees so close all of the time? What's the deal? Does he feel like he needs to monitor you guys or something? Maybe this guy is like, kind of 'whacked out' you know. Maybe it's some kind of a weird cult, and he's going to tell everyone to set their houses on fire, or poison their kids, or you know some kind of nutty . . ."

My father stood, his face white with rage. Had I known what was to come in the next few months, I could have weathered this easily. But here, now, this was the limit of my experience with fear, and I was scared. Very scared. He was looking at Troy with an ominous glare that made my insides turn to jelly. His entire body began to tremble. Gram moved quickly to Troy's chair and stood behind it placing her arms protectively around his chest. I could see her hands quivering, but her eyes were blazing. She was going to challenge him.

Chapter Two

"Chip," she began, "he has a right to ask questions. You're talking about taking him from the only home he's ever known. His friends, his school . . ."

My father, who only moments before had grinned with delight as he began to tell us of all Mr. Eden would do for us, suddenly knocked his chair backwards with such force and speed that all I heard was the shattering of glass as the china cabinet doors released their panes in what seemed like a cry of resistance.

My mother put her hand to her mouth and ran from the room. It was clear that she knew something was going to happen that would be beyond her control. A year ago my mother would have stood her ground in an argument, but a year ago she wasn't hiding bottles of gin behind the Fruit Loops.

My father advanced on Troy and Gram slowly. His eyes were narrow slits through which all of the world's evils seemed about to escape. There seemed to be no sound in the room. I'm not sure how many times the phone rang before I heard it, but I knew at once what to do.

"Dad." He didn't stop. "Dad . . . the phone. It might be Mr. Eden." He stopped cold. "Doesn't he usually call around this time?" The phone rang again. "I don't think Mom's gonna get it, Dad." Another ring. If he didn't answer it soon, the machine would pick it up. At last, this ordeal which seemed to last for hours but really took only seconds came to a halt as he turned toward the kitchen to answer the call.

Troy had a pretty good build for a ninth grader, but he didn't look very big right now. He looked at Gram. "What was he going to do?" His voice sounded small. It's puzzling that we sometimes ask questions we don't really want the answers to. This was that kind of question, and my grandmother was smart enough to know it.

"Why don't you boys come on a run with me. I've got to keep training or Mrs. Petrillo will beat me to the finish line. I'm not going to give her the satisfaction – and you two aren't going to let me. Come on now."

Troy got up from the table, but I stayed put. I wasn't afraid for me, and I wanted to hear some of my father's conversation.

"Jack," Gram rested her hand on my shoulder, "let's head outside for a while."

"I'm okay, Gram, really. You guys go ahead. I'll catch up with you. I don't want Dad to be alone right now." The last part was a lie, but it sounded noble enough. They left, though Gram reminded me that she had "bionic ears" and would hear me if I called out to her. I watched as she turned up her hearing aid to level ten. Gram's hearing was the only part of her body that seemed to show the typical signs of aging. She didn't let it get her down though. Now I used my own rather regular ears to hone in on my father's phone conversation. To listen to his voice, you would never guess that only moments ago he was behaving like a man intent on doing some bodily harm to one of his sons.

"Why Adam, I can't thank you enough for the way you take care of us. All of us at Eden. We're so grateful." There was a pause while Mr. Eden, who called semi-regularly at this time of night just to "check in" with Dad, continued his end of the conversation.

"The family? Oh, they *loved* the idea. Yes, yes. Couldn't get them to stop talking about it at dinner. The boys are thrilled at the prospect of a new school. Jack, of course, is so acquiescent that I knew he'd jump on board right away, but Troy surprised me. He's quite excited about the chance to start over somewhere new. Oh, don't worry about Troy, Adam. I'm sure you won't be disappointed with him. He's going to turn out *perfectly* – just as we discussed." My father hung up and returned to the dining room. He picked up his chair and righted it, ignoring the shards of broken glass. Then, he sat and began to eat. After a moment he spoke.

"That was Mr. Eden."

I jumped at the sound of his voice. "Oh." I said. I was grasping for words.

"We *are* moving to Paradise, Jack. And you're *both* going to love it. We all will."

" . . .Well, sure Dad. I mean if it means that much to you. I guess we'll all adjust. What about Gram? Do you think she'll . . ."

My father's voice became edgy. "Your grandmother will need to think about making other arrangements. There's a retirement facility over in Johnnsburg that I believe . . ."

I couldn't stop myself. "Retirement facility! That's a *nursing* home. Gram doesn't belong someplace like that. She's your mother. You can't . . ."

"My mother is *my* affair." He slammed his fist down on the table and my milk glass started to tumble. I caught and steadied it with my right hand. "She meddles and interferes in my life just as she always has. That time is coming to an end."

I got up from the table then and flew to the back porch door which released me to freedom. I ran. And ran. I wasn't looking for Gram and Troy – didn't want to find them in fact. What was happening to my father? He had never shared the closeness with Gram that Troy and I had, but he had always wanted her with us. Family. That was his big thing. A commitment to family, a loyalty to family. His mother would never be able to say that he had not been the best son he could be – at least in his opinion. Yet now that seemed to have changed. Since he began to work for Eden, everything was changing.

Within a few days a "For Sale" sign was in our yard, and my mother was gone. Dad had sent her to Paradise to

supervise the work on our new home. He said that Mr.
Eden would be providing a cleaning service as well as
interior designers to meet with her. They would attend to
any and all details. I remember the thought striking me as
rather odd that my father had not given her a list of details
that *he* wanted taken care of – or at least if he had, he had
not mentioned it, which was uncharacteristic of him. He
prided himself on his attention to detail and typically took
advantage of every opportunity to demonstrate the
benefits of this attribute for both Troy and me. Yet, in
this instance there was no mention of it. I've added that
to a list of things I should have given more serious
attention at the time.

The nagging question of my grandmother's living
arrangements remained unresolved. To my knowledge
she had no idea of my father's plan for her to move into
the nursing home, and it *was* a nursing home, in
Johnnsburg. This concerned me greatly, because Gram
was a lifeline for both Troy and me. I didn't tell Troy
about Dad's plan for fear that he would bring more
trouble upon himself. Besides, he was busy preparing for
a big wrestling meet – wrestling was the only sport my
brother hadn't been kicked out of for suggesting more
effective ways to drill the teams during practices.
Actually, he probably *had* made suggestions, but Coach
Schmidt liked him and tended to give him more leeway
than most adults. And Troy was coming into a good time
in his life. His grades were respectable, nowhere near as
good as mine, but decent. And he was certainly getting

attention in the girl department. Not only does Troy challenge adults, but he also has a way of challenging girls – it's a good kind of challenge, almost magnetic. They're drawn to him. Gram says it helps that he has perfect teeth, deep-set emerald green eyes, and a dark complexion. It was not uncommon to see people on the street stop and take a second look because, as Gram says, "That Troy is handsomer than all get-out." She tells me that I'm "ruggedly good-looking." When I compare our success in the girl department, though, I think I would prefer being "handsomer than all get-out."

Keeping Dad's plans for Gram a secret from Troy left me in a bit of a lurch. I relied on his input when problems arose because he always seemed to find some clever way around what I saw as a total blockade. However, if he found out what Dad was planning to do with Gram, the fireworks in our house would really be dramatic, so I stewed over my grandmother's situation alone for the first two days after the house went up for sale. And then, a resolution came. Troy was at wrestling practice and would likely be home late, so Gram and I had gone for an after-school run. I was improving – only .5 seconds behind her. We returned home and to our surprise, my father was waiting for us. He *always* arrived home at 6:00 P.M. My watch showed 5:00 P.M.

"Jack, why don't you head on upstairs and wash up for dinner. I'd like to speak with your grandmother in private." I knew where this conversation was going to go, and I did *not* want to leave. Still, something told me that

I had best do as he said. I think it was the look in his eye when he sensed my hesitation. Yes. It was the look in his eye.

Gram followed my father into his study, and I heard the heavy doors close firmly. I raced over, lay down on the floor, and pressed my ear to the opening between the floor and the base of the doors.

"Mother, the house has sold, and we'll be moving in a few days."

"Sold? Already? But it's only been on the market for two days! Who's the buyer, Chip? I hope it's a nice couple with children."

"The buyer doesn't *concern* you, Mother. I wanted to discuss your living accommodations. I've looked into a room in Johnnsburg at the . . ."

She cut him off. "Johnnsburg? Why you must be joking! That's a place for *old* people. I've no intention of going to Johnnsburg. I go where Jack and Troy go. You'll just have to see to it that there's a room for me in your swanky new home. I'm sure Mr. *Eden* wouldn't want you to throw your poor old mother out onto the street, now would he, Dear?"

"You are far from poor, Mother. It's time that you separate from these boys. Their attachment to you is . . . *unnatural*. They need to . . ."

That really fired her up. She advanced on him rapidly, and then I heard a sound that left me astonished. It was the sound of a hand striking flesh with surprising force. It was my grandmother's hand and my father's face. "How *dare* you say such a thing to me? My relationship with my grandsons is beautiful. It is not *unnatural.* Don't you ever say such a callous thing to me again." Her voice became accusatory as it rose in pitch. "It's so like you, Chip, to take something meaningful and make it sound so . . . sordid – simply because you can't understand it. This *yearning* you have for power, for . . . perfection – that's what is unnatural." The longer my grandmother talked, the more she reminded me of stories I'd heard about wild animals who become cornered. They become dangerous very quickly. "Now I don't know who this Mr. Eden is or what he's done to persuade you to uproot your family and go traipsing off to a city he basically owns, but I'll tell you this – I've got the money and the determination to fight you, Chip, and I will. You try and separate the boys from me, and I'll see that Mr. Eden's name is headlining newspapers in every town within a fifty-mile radius! Now, why is it I have a suspicion he wouldn't like that? No, Chip, the only way you'll get these boys to *Paradise* without me is to go straight through Hell." And with that, she walked to the door, paused a moment before opening it so that I had time to get up and out of the way, and then proceeded quite calmly out into the foyer and up to her room.

Chapter Three

There is an aroma in the gym at Central High that the word offensive doesn't begin to describe. The kids say that the sweat from gym classes and athletic games over the past ninety-three years has embedded itself in the wood floor which now emits this rank odor at thirty-two second intervals. Add to it the perspiring bodies of wrestlers in grades 9-12 from two area high schools and you've found the perfect spot for an air freshener company to make a major pitch. Yet, Gram and I were seated in our usual spots oblivious to the smell due to our excitement over Troy's record-breaking season. I was experiencing a heightened awareness of my mother's absence as she always sat on the other side of me at the meets. One thing about my mother – she never missed any event that either Troy or I participated in, until now. I reminded myself that she was busy preparing the new house for our arrival and that she would be here otherwise, but something was troubling me. Why hadn't she called us? She knew Troy's big meet was today. Her drinking hadn't been interfering with her performance in the family, so I found it hard to imagine that she had been so completely sauced for the past few days that she didn't think of us. I decided to ask Dad about it when I got home and turned to see what Gram thought of the idea when she grabbed my hand with excitement. "Here comes your bro, Jackie-boy!" she said enthusiastically.

Troy was making his way out onto the mat, as was his opponent, the lead wrestler in his division from Nicholson High. Gram held up a rose and softly blew on it until a petal released and began floating down the bleachers. Don't ask me why, but it was a tradition. Gram always brought a rose to special events, and she always blew on it until one petal was released. When she got home, she'd press the remainder of the rose and write the date and event underneath it in one of her many scrapbooks. I was thinking that I should ask her for a more detailed explanation regarding this tradition of hers when I noticed something peculiar. A man in a black trench coat and hat was standing near the sidelines with a video camera aimed at the wrestling mat. His hat was pulled down so far that it shielded his face; however, I could see a red light glowing – indicating that filming was taking place. After watching his camera for several minutes, one thing was clear – he was filming my brother!

My mind was racing with questions. College coach – looking to offer scholarships? No. Troy was in ninth grade. Perhaps this man was the father of the boy Troy was wrestling. Certainly. That must be it. And to think I had almost worried Gram by mentioning it to her. And yet, after Troy won the match, rather quickly I might add, I saw the man walk to the opposite side of the gym and remove a large camera with what looked like a major zoom lens. It followed Troy's every movement as he headed back to the bench. Although I couldn't hear it, I knew instinctively that the shutter was clicking almost continuously.

"Let's go, Gram." I tried to keep the desperation out of my voice. "Let's take Troy with us, too."

"Why, Jack, the meet isn't even finished. Don't you want to see some of the other boys?"

I had to play this right or she would become suspicious. "Well, I do . . . but we only have a few more days left in town, and I'm kind of sad. Being here makes me sad, and Troy's probably ready, anyway. He never stays for the team parties."

She reached for her purse. "Whatever you say, kiddo. You go grab your brother, and I'll get the car. See you out front."

"Right." I said. I headed down the bleachers two at a time. The man in the coat was nowhere in sight, and I wasn't sure if I was glad about that or not. Somehow I kind of liked knowing where he was. Of course, Troy was completely obstinate about leaving the meet.

"What are you – nuts? Why should I walk out of a major meet when there are three guys left to go?" He was eyeing me suspiciously. My brother is very perceptive.

I had to get him out of that gym, and I knew just the way to do it. "Gram started feeling dizzy, Troy. I'm worried." Bingo! He grabbed his duffel bag, ran over to notify Coach Schmidt that he was leaving, and after that it was all I could do to keep up with him.

"She's feeling dizzy, and you let her go to the car alone? Jack, you moron, what's the matter with you!"

"Lost my head," I countered. He wasn't really mad – just concerned. My brother and I don't argue. The last time we had a fight of any real proportion was when he boiled my G.I. Joe in vegetable oil. Third grade. Like Gram says – he has a bit of the devil in him.

The ride home kept me very busy. It's not easy to direct and control the conversation of two people so that they don't figure out that you've been "storytelling." Gram says it's only *lying* when it's done with malicious intent; otherwise, it's storytelling. Well, there was one story I *wasn't* telling, not yet anyway. And that one had a character I couldn't identify except for his hat and coat.

My decision to keep quiet about the man at the gym put me in an awkward position. If I wasn't going to tell anyone, including my brother, that someone might be watching him, I was going to have to keep him under heavy-duty surveillance myself. Luckily, we had only two days left until the big move, and while the days were relatively uneventful, the nights were another story. They say that when you try to bury things, they always find a way to the surface. Well, my buried fears regarding Troy's unidentified fan were creating dark circles under my eyes. The past two nights had found me bolting awake at hours of the night when I normally exhibit a posture close to that of a corpse. On each occasion my sheets were soaked in sweat, and I was in possession of a vivid nightmare in which my brother had been kidnapped and was being mercilessly tortured. He was crying out for me, but I could not find him. And a clock always seemed to be ticking in the background – symbolizing that I was running out of time.

Added to the delightful antics of my dreamworld, there was my conversation starter at dinner regarding the absence of a call from my mother. My father seemed to miss the cue that this was supposed to lead to a discussion, so Troy helped out.

"Dad, didn't you hear Jack? What's up with Mom not checking in? Seems a little *odd* don't you think?"

My father wiped the corners of his mouth with his napkin and placed his fork down on his plate so that it made a noise. It seemed to me that he wanted it to make a noise though I can't imagine why. "Troy, I'm growing weary of your comments regarding things being bizarre or odd with regard to our *corporate family*. Mr. Eden is seeing to it that we have the best of everything, and if you can't show a little gratitude, you could at least keep quiet. Especially given his particular interest in you." He regretted saying it the minute it was out of his mouth. Not because he was afraid it would in some way trouble *me*, but because we weren't supposed to know. It was written all over his face.

Gram stopped chewing immediately and regarded Dad with a look of suspicion.

"Huh?" For being as intelligent as he was, Troy was a bit naive at times. "What do you mean *particular interest?*"

"Mr. Eden came to your wrestling meet the other night. He was extremely impressed with what he saw. He's declared himself a big fan of yours. That's all. You should feel honored." My father began eating again. Rapidly.

The butterflies in my stomach threatened to bring my entire meal back up. There was no doubt in my mind that Mr. Eden was the man who had been filming and photographing Troy at that meet. But why?

"The guy comes to my meet and doesn't even introduce himself, and I'm supposed to feel honored?" Troy was saddling up to ride a dangerous trail. "Well, maybe I *should* feel honored, you know." His voice began to exude a sarcastic edge. "I believe it's the first time an adult male has ever attended one of my meets."

The silence was deafening. It was as if we all sat frozen in time. I was prepared for an explosion just below nuclear, but my father surprised me. In one smooth motion, he placed his fork beside his plate, rose from his chair in preparation to exit the room, looked at Troy and retorted evenly, "Mr. Eden is *very* impressed with you. Lucky for you."

It was much later that evening when I realized something. Dad never did answer our question about Mom.

Chapter Four

"Well, that's the last of it. Come on, Jackie! Let's go get the rest of the gang, and then we're on our way!"

Talk about two people at opposite ends of the spectrum. I was watching, ruefully, as the moving van turned the corner of Vine Street carrying the last seventeen years of my life with it, and my father was acting like a kid with a new box of crayons. His exuberance was unrestrained. How could he be so excited about leaving the house he and Mom had lived in most of their married life? The house that had hosted countless school sleepovers at which no one slept. The house that Troy nearly burned to the ground when he was eight.

Mom said she and Dad were having coffee one morning when they repeatedly heard the patter of Troy's little bare feet racing from the bathroom to his bedroom and back again. This continued for what they decided was far too long and when they went upstairs to investigate, they found their younger son had started a small fire in his bedroom closet. He had been running back and forth from the bathroom to the closet with a Dixie cup of water trying to put out the flames.

There were memories in this house. How could my father be so insensitive? After all, this was the house *his* father, my Grampa Amos, had died in.

"I'll get Troy and Gram," I said heading into the house. No point in subjecting them to "Mr. Good Time" when I was sure they were feeling as nostalgic as I was. I took solace in the fact that no further discussion had taken place regarding Gram's living arrangements. Apparently, the tongue-lashing she'd given my father had done the trick. Or her threat to fight him.

My grandmother has been a very wealthy woman for most of her adult life. She has never been one to *flaunt* her money – although she does have a habit of splurging on clothes and shoes. She has always wanted to look good, and it just seems that the brand names look best on her. And she does like to ride in style. She sold her motorcycle last year (too many speeding tickets) and settled on some new foreign sports car. Fire engine red with a white interior – gotta love it. She gives generously to charities both locally and around the world, and she does volunteer work for the Red Cross. She's worked at the soup kitchen downtown and has served on the library board. She has also coordinated the community Christmas dinner for the past two years – a task she has undertaken with less than her typical enthusiasm.

"I can't believe it!" She told us after her day in traffic court. She'd been summoned there after receiving her third speeding ticket in eighteen months. "Greg Dreyer, that young pup of a judge, assigned me to co-chair the community Christmas dinner for the next two years with *Ethel Wifflebaum* – imagine *me* working with *Ethel*! She's about as much fun as a fever blister. Dreyer says it's my community service for what he calls an 'inordinate number of traffic violations'!" I asked him if he'd ever opened up a motorcycle out on the road and been able to slow her down at every little speed limit sign, but I don't guess he wanted to tackle that subject." She looked across the table at us and winked. "Boys, remind me not to vote for him when he's up for re-election."

The people in our town knew Gram for who she was, and they adored her – even Judge Dreyer, who sent her an invitation to dinner at a posh restaurant a week after he sentenced her. It was also common knowledge in our town that Gram had money. She and my Grampa Amos started their own printing company in this town over fifty years ago. It grew and grew until it became a corporation employing several hundred people. In all those years, my grandparents made it their policy to know every employee personally. They walked through the press rooms and talked to the men and women working on the presses, even in the heat of July and August. They had the secretarial staff over for dinner. Gram sent birthday cards to employees and flowers to new mothers when babies were born. Grampa talked with the people. He asked them how he could improve their working conditions, and then he responded. I remember the giant thank you card they sent him when he added water coolers throughout the plant and giant fans to move the air around in the press rooms a bit. Anyone who knew my grandparents could understand why the employees at AK Printing never unionized; there was no need.

When Grampa Amos died, Gram turned the day-to-day operations of the company over to Bill Simpson, who had been my grandfather's most trusted friend for nearly his entire life. They had been friends since grade school, and Bill had served as the company Vice-President for over two decades before Grampa's death. Gram retained controlling interest in the company's stock, served as Chairman of the Board, and saw to it that the people were treated much as they'd always been. That's why they loved her so. In addition, as sole owner of such a successful corporation, her "salary" was sizable to say the least. Those two realities, her money and her popularity, made her both a powerful ally and a formidable enemy – and my father knew it.

He had never shown the slightest interest in the printing industry – at least not that I was aware of. He thought my grandparents were foolish. I remember him discussing the situation with my mother as we drove to the country club for Sunday lunch one afternoon. "Susan," he explained. "They can't continue to run that corporation with a small town mentality. They could be making triple the profits they're currently generating."

My mother adored Gram and Grampa, so I knew she didn't agree with Dad. Still, her response was weighed carefully. "I don't know, Chip. I think it's sweet the way they care so much for the employees. Look at how low

the turnover rate is! The employees are incredibly loyal –
no one wants to quit working there. Your parents seem to
be quite successful financially. How do you know they
could improve their profit margin?"

"I've met with an accountant and a corporate attorney,
and they both say that my parents are not . . ."

"Chip!" She was aghast. "You had no right to do
that. I don't want to hear any of this. This is none of our
affair."

"I have an interest in this, Susan. Who do you think
they'll be leaving that business to when they pass on? It's
only right that I take an interest in the way they manage
it."

"But you've always said you want nothing to do with
it," she countered.

"I don't – now. But when they leave it to me, I'm
going to sell it. I haven't the time or the inclination to run
a 'Mom and Pop' business. Besides, I don't want people
saying I built my career off of my parents. Still, the way
they handle their business affairs today *will* impact its
salability later on. I just want to keep an eye on things."

"Please, Chip." she touched his hand gently. "Don't
bring this up today. Your parents are so wonderful to us.
Let's not spoil the afternoon." She looked at him through
pleading green eyes – then brushed her auburn hair back
behind her ears. I watched all of this from the back seat
knowing that she would win and that he would be silent.
In those days my mother rarely drank liquor of any kind.
She was extremely health conscious and incredibly

lovely. Back then my father melted almost on command, but since he had gone to work for Eden, he seemed to find fault with her almost constantly. And she began to drink frequently – hard liquor – the kind that wears on people. It was only a matter of time until the effects of the booze would begin to tarnish her appearance.

"Troy! Gram!" I hollered down the basement stairs, but there was no response. I had already checked the entire first floor, so the second floor quickly became a most attractive option. I jumped on the first step, preparing to bolt upwards at breakneck speed as Troy and I were accustomed to doing, when my brother appeared at the top of the staircase and raised his hand to quiet me. His face was grim.

"Not now, bro," was all he said.

I soft-shoed the staircase and found him standing at the double-door entrance to Gram's room. Actually, her "room" was really an enormous apartment – kind of a penthouse suite, except for the fact that there were three other bedrooms on this level of the house. She and Grampa had designed the apartment themselves and, of course, paid for everything when it was decided they would come to live with us in the new house my parents were building. I never understood why they chose to live under the same roof with Dad. He loved them, I suppose, out of sense of duty, but if he *liked* them, it was the world's best-kept secret.

"Amos," it was my grandmother's voice. "I have to leave you now. We spent our best years in this house. You always said that. Remember when we decided to come here? I told you, 'Amos, we can take care of ourselves. What do we want to go moving in with Chip and Susan for? People in town will talk. They'll say we're getting *old*. They'll say we're not giving our son and his family the privacy they need. They'll say we're thoughtless and inconsiderate and who knows what all!' And you said, 'Katy, the people of this fine town love us, and we love them. But do you know who I love more? My grandsons. And I'll gladly tolerate the gossip around town if it means I can spend one extra minute of my life with those boys. We won't crowd them, and we won't shadow them. But . . . we're going to be here for them any time they need us.'"

Her voice began to take on a vulnerability that neither Troy nor I had ever heard. "Oh, Amos, you were so right. So right about the boys, so right about coming here to live, so right about everything. Did I tell you that often enough? I hope so."

I heard her heels clicking on the hardwood floors as she paced the three generous rooms of their apartment. I don't believe she knew we were waiting just outside the doorway, and we probably should have distanced ourselves. This was clearly eavesdropping on a very intimate moment. Yet, we both seemed riveted to the floor. Gram had told us a lot of stories through the years but never this one.

"Well, Amos, my *best* friend and love – those boys you wanted to be here for are leaving today, and I've been forced to make a decision. Go with them or stay with you, here. Here. In this house where my fondest memories of you are. And Amos, forgive me . . . but I have to go." At that moment her voice cracked, and we heard sobs racking through a body that for the first time in my life looked fragile. I moved toward the doorway, but Troy held me back. I looked into his eyes and saw a flood of emotion making its way forward, and the next thing I knew we were embracing our grandmother in the empty shell of some rooms that had held a deeper meaning for her than we had ever guessed. After a few moments, she seemed to regain her strength and moved to a built-in shelf near her bedroom. On top lay one of her scrapbooks and a rose. She picked up the rose and walked toward the window. "Tradition," she said and her eyes danced even as they began to tear over again.

"Where in the *hell* have you been?" His voice shook with rage, and his footsteps were weighted as if his shoes were made of lead. As my father approached us, I noticed that the veins and blood vessels on his neck looked ready to pop open and shower us in blood and whatever other kind of gunk was inside there. "I have been downstairs waiting for nearly fifteen minutes. Fifteen minutes – wasted! While the three of you are doing God knows what in an *empty* house!" Then, his eyes fell on the rose in Gram's hand. "*You.*" He forced the word out with such disdain that I was shocked. I couldn't believe my father was speaking this way. He sounded almost inhuman. "I should have known it would have something to do with you! I hope you're happy, Mother. Mr. Eden is expecting us in far less time than we now have to arrive in Paradise which means that we will be LATE! *LATE TO MEET MR. EDEN!*" He was shrieking – almost hysterical. I couldn't breathe. "And for what? Some idiotic tradition of yours!" He had the flower in his hand before I knew what to do, and it was crushed beneath his heel before I knew what to say. But not my brother. Troy knew what to do. As for what to say – the best he could muster was a cry of fury as he launched himself at our father. The right hook would have leveled me, and I'm two years older than Troy, but it only drew blood from my father's nose and seemed to unsteady him for a moment. Troy came at him again, but my father, an avid wrestler in his day, caught Troy and had him to the ground in less than a minute. He placed Troy in a choke hold, at least I think that's what it's called, and it looked as though my brother was struggling for air. I was sure of it when his feet began to kick wildly. And then, almost too coincidentally, my father's pager sounded. He released Troy roughly, glanced hurriedly at his pager, and his face became panic stricken. He bolted from the room with no further comment.

Gram and I rushed to Troy and helped him sit up. He was gasping for air, and it took a few minutes for his breathing to return to normal. "All right, boys, that's enough. We *are* leaving but not with your father."

"Gram, we have to go with him. What about Mom? We haven't heard from her at all. I'm worried. Dad's obviously way over the stress limit, but maybe things will be okay once we're in the new house. It seems so important to him that we go there." I was actually trying to convince all three of us.

The clearing of his throat startled us. We looked toward the doorway, and there he stood. The blood from his nose was wiped clean and there were no visible signs that only moments ago his powerful hands had been locked around my brother's throat. "Mr. Eden was worried about us," was all my father said.

Chapter Five

I've heard of gated communities where every well-to-do family has well-to-do neighbors on either side, but Paradise was in a class all by itself. It wasn't a gated community; it was a gated village! As we approached the entrance, enormous brick columns – 10 to12 feet tall with wrought-iron fencing seemed to encapsulate the land for as far as the eye could see. The landscape beyond the entrance was a Monet come to life. Through the opening at the gatehouse we could view a magnificent lake with water as clear and blue as the purest sapphire, and birds seemed to be singing from within the village – a thousand melodies which combined in a symphony of incomparable beauty. We could make out several varieties of flowers and trees as we drove toward the gatehouse, and it seemed a certainty that even more wonders awaited us within.

And then I saw it – a large sign with brass letters that were tarnished and cracked in several places welcoming visitors with a simple phrase: *You are now entering Paradise.* The simplicity of the words and the shoddy condition of the sign were in marked contrast to the lavishness which existed just a few meters beyond, and the longer I looked at it – the more out of place it seemed. Something about that sign bothered me.

While Gram and Troy gawked in childlike wonder at the majesty before them, and I wrestled with my neurosis over the welcome sign, Dad appeared to be taking the whole thing in stride. He pulled up to the gatehouse as if he were stopping at a roadside tollbooth, but the creature who leaned out to greet him didn't look like any toll collector I had ever seen.

If my heart didn't stop beating at that moment, then it must have reached a palpitation level that was beyond the speed of light because I couldn't feel it, nor could I seem to regulate my respirations which were coming in short gasps. Everything before my eyes seemed to be rapidly going in and out of focus.

I was looking at the most beautiful girl in the world. She smiled and I thought I might just die right then and there from the shock of seeing her move: it proved she was alive. This was good. Girls who were alive could go out with boys who were alive. And the electricity moving through my hormonally charged body assured me that I was indeed very much alive at that moment. In fact, I began to question if I had ever truly been alive until I saw her smile.

My father rolled down the car window.

"Good afternoon, Mr. . . . ."

"Jori!" He cut into her greeting with surprising curtness, took the clipboard of paperwork she offered him, and began to write with great haste. It seemed to me that this girl made him nervous. She made me nervous, too, but I don't think it was for the same reason. While I credited Dad for acknowledging her name – it's nice of places to provide nametags so people can be a bit more sociable – I felt that his interrupting her was both inexcusable and insensitive. Hopefully, she wouldn't generalize that kind of impolite behavior to his sons. No, make that *son*. Singular was best in these situations. Unfortunately, God granted my brother the privilege of having vision as finely attuned as mine, and *he* was on the left side, which in this case was the *right* side, of the car.

He rolled his window down expeditiously and unloaded. "Now I know why they call this place *Paradise*," he said as he displayed the grin that had, at one time or another, broken the heart of nearly every female who had come within proximity of it. "I'm Troy, but if you don't like that name I'll change it."

I was about to be sick. Very sick.

Gram leaned forward toward the front passenger seat and poked my ribs. "He's gotta get better material, Jack. Where's he get this stuff?"

"Beats me, Gram," I muttered. The frustrating thing was, it worked. Fabulously. Consistently. Without fail. *Except* . . . on this girl.

"Where do you get those cheesy pick-up lines?" she countered good-naturedly. And then she looked past Troy and up to the front of the car. "Do *you* have a name?"

In jumped Troy. "Who – him? Oh, he's . . . Oooouuuch! Hey! Owww!"

Gram was fast. She spoke softly enough so that only Troy and I could hear her but firmly enough so that *he* got her message. "Troy – my love, quiet down. Now Grandma has manipulated your pinky finger into a rather uncomfortable position at this moment for a reason. You see, Dear, you've just come down with a severe case of laryngitis, and I'm afraid you won't be capable of talking again until we are out of this charming young lady's domain. Nod if you understand, and I'll release your finger." Gram reached through the middle of the front seats and elbowed me with her free arm. "Now would be a good time to speak to the girl, Dear."

"Huh? Oh, yeah. Uhhhh. Jerk . . . I mean Jack. Yeah, Jack. That's my name all right. I'm Jack. Yes sir, that's what they call me, Jack." Pause. I sounded like a complete idiot. "And you're Janice, right?"

"Jori." She grinned at me and my brain screamed at my lungs to inhale. "Oh, yeah . . . right. I should have paid better attention to your name tag."

"That's okay. It's not a very common name. Besides, I'm not wearing a nametag. We don't even have them here, but your fath . . ."

All of a sudden the car shifted violently into gear, and we were moving toward the electronic arm of the gatehouse far too quickly. He hit the brakes, the tires squealed, and we came to an abrupt halt. The arm rested comfortably on our windshield. "Oops!" Dad remarked. "I forgot to leave my paperwork at the gatehouse."

I was still reeling from the jolt, but I wasn't going to miss an opportunity like this. Gram's warning look held Troy in check. "I'll run the paperwork back to her," I said in my best Eagle Scout voice. Troy never made it to Eagle Scout. His idea of a service project was offering to revise the National Scouting Handbook so that it was more "user friendly." He sent a sample chapter to the chairman of the National Scouting Organization who returned it saying that neither Troy's limericks nor the pictures from *Today's Hottest Teen Girls* magazine were appropriate for a scouting handbook. He also suggested that *perhaps* Troy wasn't cut out for Eagle Scouts just yet.

Dad opened his car door and stepped out.

Perhaps he hadn't heard me. "Dad, *I'll* be glad to take her the papers." I was trying not to seem too excited at the prospect of returning to the gatehouse, but apparently he saw through my charade.

"*I* will be delivering these papers, Jack. You can forget about her, son. *She* doesn't belong in Paradise."

Chapter Six

I have no way of knowing how long we had been driving through the streets of Paradise before we arrived at our new home because I was lost in thought. My father's firm disapproval of a girl who was making my heart do somersaults was occupying one portion of my conscious mind while my remaining brain cells were devoted to determining if what I was seeing as we drove through this village could actually be real. *Paradise* appeared to be everything its name indicated.

The streets and sidewalks were immaculate; there was no evidence of trash or litter anywhere. Some special type of stone had been used to build the sidewalks, and it was obvious that whatever it was – it was expensive. In addition, the sidewalks were bordered by intricate brickwork with large planters of flowers located every so many feet. Each flower was in full bloom. Every business we passed was impressive and well maintained on the outside, and I suspected that the insides would yield a similar sense of decorum. The downtown bustled with people, all of whom appeared to be experiencing an enjoyable afternoon. Every face registered a sense of contentment and peace. It was almost eerie. On second thought, it wasn't *almost* eerie, it was *totally* eerie.

As we left the downtown area and made our way through several neighborhoods, I noted an extremely large facility located at a higher elevation than the rest of the village. Sunlight cascaded over an enormous roof that looked as though it was made of gold. Was such a thing possible? I didn't know, but it was clearly designed to impress . . . or *intimidate*. The outside walls appeared to be made entirely of glass, yet I couldn't be sure because it was pretty far away. The building towered above every visible structure in the village, but despite its magnificence, I had a sense of foreboding about it. It seemed to have an ominous presence all its own, almost as if it were alive.

"Hey, Dad, what's that big building off to the right?" I asked. Perhaps striking up a conversation would improve his mood.

"That, gentlemen and *young* lady," he eyed Gram through the rearview mirror as he complimented her, "is *Eden* – the finest corporation in the world!" He was clearly pleased that I had inquired about this building. He was practically gushing with a pride that he could hardly contain which led me to wonder if he was developing some kind of a bipolar personality disorder. One minute he was furious, and the next he was almost perky.

"Aaahh," Troy dramatically smacked his forehead with his hand and retorted in the petulant tone he reserves for adults he wants to tick off. "I should have guessed! *What* else could that building have been? Now, Jack, what's wrong with you, boy? Don't you know God's gift to the corporate world when you see it?"

I cringed and waited for my father's bellow of rage, but he remained silent. I could tell by looking at his back that he had tensed, but for some reason he was going to let it go this time. Troy's "anti-Eden" attitude had obviously been solidified during the wrestling match before we left home. Troy didn't like to lose.

"Chip, this can't be. You can't be serious." Gram's voice echoed my sense of disbelief. My father had just turned onto a brick driveway that snaked between two awesome alabaster pillars topped with beautiful lights. The driveway was at least a quarter of a mile long and was leading us to our new home and *that* was the problem. This wasn't a house. This was a mansion – solid brick and what looked to be three stories high; it was the most beautiful home I had ever seen. No movie star had a house that was even in the same ballpark as this. It was beyond description.

My father responded with what was clearly fake humility. He couldn't keep the pride out of his voice. "Yes, Mother, I'm serious. *This* is our new house. It's the kind of house we should have been living in all along. Well boys, what do you think? Pretty impressive, huh?"

We were dumbfounded. I decided it was probably best that Troy was speechless, so I popped out an answer to keep the waters calm. "It's really something, Dad. How did you afford it? I mean our old house was nice and all, but this makes it seem like we were living in a trailer before."

"Jack, when Mr. Eden is happy with you, there's no end to the good things that will come your way. You remember that now." He looked in the rearview mirror – directly at my brother – as he said, "Both of you."

The movers were busily placing our furnishings about the house as we entered. They appeared to have maps that provided the information on "what went where," and we were completely disregarded. They reminded me of worker bees. Fast and focused. I never heard a grunt or groan as they moved the heaviest objects. None of them even stopped for a break or a drink – at least not that I saw. If given enough time, I would have grown more suspicious of this herd of "He-Men," but suddenly, I realized what was *really* missing from this house. "Where's Mom?" It came out loud. It came out in a voice that bordered on accusation, and I immediately felt a need to soften it. "I figured she'd be here directing traffic."

Dad instantly picked up his briefcase and jingled his car keys. "Oh. Didn't I tell you? I thought I told you yesterday. I certainly meant to. Well, with so much excitement around here, you can hardly blame me. Your mother is attending a special retreat for the wives of some of Mr. Eden's 'top brass.'" He looked at Gram, "Mother, it was *you* that I told. You said you'd informed the boys already."

"Chip, you never said anything to me about Susan not being . . ."

He cut her off. "Oh, Mother, don't feel bad. You're allowed to forget a thing or two at your age. It's not any big deal. The boys can survive without their mother for a while – right fellas?"

I could see a storm brewing in Troy's eyes. "Sure, Dad," I said with a glance at Troy and Gram. "How long will she be gone?"

"Well, let's see. She just left a couple of hours ago – that's why I was so upset that we were running late. I knew she wouldn't want to miss seeing you two before she left. I think the retreat is running about four days. Of course, she could decide to come home early, or you never know, she could decide to stay an extra week. Listen, I've got to run to the office. You guys check out the new place, and your grandmother will take care of dinner." He looked at Gram. "Mother, be sure they get some rest. Tomorrow they'll be registering at their new school." He delivered the entire speech in this sickeningly sweet tone that only further convinced me that he was lying, but he was out the door and gone before I could say anymore. Good thing, too, because Troy blew an instant later.

"Wives' retreat – right. Yeah. Sure. We're supposed to believe that? I don't! Not for a New York minute. Gram, what's going on here? Where's Mom? How can he afford this house?" The longer Troy talked the more hyper he became.

Gram stepped forward and in her best "take charge" voice said, "Boys, I don't know where your mother is, but we're going to find out. Carefully. First, let's all find rooms upstairs – from the size of this Taj Mahal there must be plenty of choices. I want you to get settled in, and then we'll meet for dinner and a big pow-wow."

Troy and I agreed and headed upstairs with our suitcases in tow. We would have carried Gram's things, but she gets mad when you ask. If it's her idea, it's fine; otherwise, keep quiet and leave her alone.

After searching through several bedrooms for the twin beds Troy and I had always shared, it became clear that they had been left behind or sold without our input. Unlike most siblings, Troy and I never wanted our own rooms. We'd always had a room large enough that we each had our own "space." There were times that it didn't work so well, but on the whole we both preferred it. We talked a lot in the evenings. I think it's one of the things that has given us a close relationship. We're brothers, but we're also friends. Anyway, it was obvious that in *this* house, we were to have separate rooms. I was feeling very uneasy about being separated from Troy; moreover, Gram settled on a room at the far end of the hall because of the view. I wished she hadn't chosen a room so far away from ours, but I didn't have a good reason for asking her to move. How does a junior in high school tell his grandmother he's afraid of . . . well, that was the problem. I didn't even know exactly what I was afraid of – but I was afraid of something.

By the time Troy and I finished unpacking and setting up, a delicious aroma was wafting up the stairs from the kitchen. It smelled like Chinese! Troy looked at me and grinned mischievously. "Gram's been hard at work as usual!"

I grinned back. "Some things never change!" We both raced out of the room and down the stairs – eager more to verify our prediction than for the food. Sure enough, we were right.

Gram sat at the table already beginning to play with her chopsticks. There were several bags with white cardboard containers sitting all around the table. "Hey, fellas! What took you so long? *Darn* these things!" Gram tossed her chopsticks into one of the empty bags. "I'll never quit trying to use them, but life's short. I can only invest so much time in them."

Troy and I pulled up our chairs and laughed. Two constants in our universe, it seemed, would remain certain even in Paradise. Number one: whenever Gram was supposed to make our dinner, she would order out. Number two: seventy-five percent of the time she would order Chinese, try to use the chopsticks for a few minutes, and then pitch them back into the sack and grab a fork. Although our conversation at dinner remained lighthearted, I think we all knew what was coming. We were simply avoiding it. It's interesting that people do those things. Avoid what makes them uncomfortable and yet they're uncomfortable the whole time they're avoiding it. That was definitely the case in this instance.

Soon, we retired to Gram's room for a "pow-wow" as she called it. Upon entering the room, I was struck by how very small it seemed. Actually, it wasn't small, but compared with the apartment she and Grampa had enjoyed in the old house, this was tiny. It was a room. Nothing remarkable. And I wondered if, while Troy and I were searching for a room with twin beds, she had looked for a commodious set of rooms somewhere that indicated she had been thought of – that her son had planned for her to come and had wanted her to have accommodations similar to what she'd always had. Or, had she not even bothered looking. Had she known she would find nothing special?

Seating herself in a camel-colored antique chair she'd had recovered a dozen times, Gram addressed us gravely. "Boys, it's time we started being up front with one another. You're too old for me to worry about speaking my mind, and I'm too young for you to worry about upsetting me. Let's lay our cards on the table. What do you say?"

Troy, never one to hesitate or mince words, spoke up. "Mom's gone, Dad's nuts, and I hate this place already. I say we confront him – threaten to call the police or something. We have to *do* something, Gram!"

"Troy darling," she bent down in the chair and gently ruffled his hair. He was seated on the floor and looked up at her with flashing eyes that revealed his restless nature. "You're as impetuous as ever, but right now we need to be careful. Your father hasn't technically done anything that we can *prove* is illegal."

"What do you call choking your kid? A paternal love-tap?"

"Stop it, Troy!" I said. "You know what Gram means. That isn't going to be enough to get us anywhere. Besides it's his word against ours. I think we need to concentrate on finding Mom. I don't believe she's at a wives' retreat either, and I'm *sure* she didn't leave two hours before we got here! She would have left us a note – something! She hasn't communicated with us since she left home to come here."

"If," Gram threw us for a curve, "she ever got here."

A chill ran down my back. My brother bolted out of the room, and I was right behind him. I knew where he was going, and I thought I knew what he would find. He burst through the double doors to the master bedroom suite and headed for the closet. I slowed a bit. I didn't want to see her side of the closet empty. No dresses. No women's shoes. I felt certain that my mother had never been in this house. Still, I didn't want him to make the discovery alone. I came up behind him just as he opened the door, and we both gasped aloud.

"YESSSS!" Troy shouted in triumph as his right fist shot victoriously skyward. But even as he began sorting through the clothes on the rack, I realized they would be hers. This had all been perfectly arranged to make us think she was in this house, but I didn't believe it. Troy, on the other hand, was desperate to believe it. I heard him in the bathroom rifling through the drawers. It was as if every indication that Mom had been physically present in this house was breathing fresh air into his oxygen-deprived lungs. He couldn't get enough assurance. He combed through her dresser and her armoire, seeming to draw more and more strength with each new find. And the longer he searched, the more I expected everything to be here, less a few items she would supposedly have taken on her trip. But she wasn't on a trip. I was certain of it.

"Boys."

Gram's voice.

She had entered the room and was holding a brass picture frame in the shape of two hearts joined in the middle. The glass was cracked. In it were pictures of Troy and me. It was our Valentine's gift to Mom when we were a couple of little squirts. Gram had helped us pick it out, but we cut out the pictures to mount them in the frame on our own. We cut them unevenly so the pictures never fit quite right, but Mom had said it was terrific. She had kept it on her bedside table for eight years with one exception – she took it with her whenever she went away. Always. Visiting her parents in Cleveland, biking with Aunt Linda on their annual vacation getaway, traveling with Dad back when he worked for Lexington. Even staying up nights in the hospital when her father, my Grampa Joe, was dying of cancer. She had been gone for several weeks then, and it went along. She never left it. Eight years. She never forgot it. Always remembered it. *Always.*

Chapter Seven

I don't know who did it or when it was done, but sometime in the night, while we slept, someone entered both Troy's room and mine.

We knew because when we woke up there were clothes laid out for us to wear to "school." Crisp white shirts that appeared to have come straight from the dry cleaners, navy blazers, tan pants – pleated, cuffed, and ironed with a perfect crease, and ties in a paisley pattern of navy and yellow. Brand new socks – tan to match the pants and shiny burgundy loafers rounded out the apparel. Upon closer inspection, I found an insignia on the pocket of the blazer that read *The Garden School*. I sighed. It appeared that Mr. Eden's school went for the uniform theory in a major way. Troy was *not* going to like this. I found the clothes to be a perfect fit, which should have seemed more incredible than it did at the time, but I was preoccupied. Jori, the beautiful girl at the gatehouse, had made a guest appearance in my dreams. I was hardly conscious of the process of dressing myself as I relived the dream in which I found a way to create coherent sentences in her presence, and she confessed that she knew she loved me from the minute our eyes met. Guys do dream things like that. We just don't tell anyone.

"One guess who looks like a department store mannequin?" Troy's teasing voice, then his eyes and that devilish grin eased slowly around the edge of the doorframe. Then, he leapt inside. "Ta Da! What do you think? Not Mr. Eden's standard attire, but I think it'll do!" I stared at my brother in amazement. He wasn't wearing any of the garments that had been laid out for him during the night. Instead, he looked like a combat officer ready for guerrilla warfare. Dark tan army boots made his feet look much larger than they were, and his camouflage pants were tucked into the boots so they puckered at the top edge. The buckle from a braided brown belt, which was far too big, hung at least two inches down from his waist. He was wearing a cream-colored sleeveless shirt, and an army green kerchief was tied tightly around his neck. His hair obviously had some kind of gel in it because it had that permanently wet look. His green eyes danced. There was mischief written all over them.

Upon seeing my brother, I involuntarily began entertaining multiple scenarios, all of them ending in disaster, as I envisioned my father coming up the stairs and seeing him.

"Well," he grinned and showed those perfect white teeth, "what do you think? Bet I'll make an impression at The Garden School – don't you think, Big Bro?"

"Troy, please." I couldn't find the words. "Can't you just do what he wants? Just for a while? Just until we

can find out about Mom? You're not going to prove
anything by making him angry."

"Hey, take it easy! Like the man said – Mr. Eden
likes me! Well, *this* is who I am! He'll probably get a
kick out of this!"

"Troy, I don't think so. Listen to me." I walked over
to my little brother and put my hands on his shoulders. I
looked him right in the eye, and I willed him with every
ounce of my being to yield – something he rarely did.
"Don't do this. *Please*."

We stood in silence for a moment. Finally, he reached
up and shoved my head to one side. "All right, you big
kiss-up. You win. But I'm telling you right now that the
girls aren't going to go for me in that get-up." He pointed
at my outfit. "Shoot! I wouldn't even go for me in that
get-up. And I know what a totally awesome guy I am!" I
breathed a sigh of relief. I had won, or so I thought.
"Think I should stop down and give Gram a chance to see
what could have been," he pointed to his attire with pride,
"before I put on the monkey suit for you?"

That's when I heard the footsteps and voice
simultaneously echoing as he headed down the hall to my
room. It was too late. We froze as he began addressing
us even before he entered the room.

"Well, gentlemen. Are you ready to meet the staff
and faculty of the most prestigious school in all of . . ."
He stopped in mid sentence as he came through the door.
His eyes looked as if they would shoot out deadly beams
and incinerate Troy where he stood. He spoke two words

into the deadly silence. They sounded as cold as ice –
almost as if, upon leaving his lips, they would freeze, then
fall and shatter on contact with the ground.

"*Get out.*"

My father's entire body trembled. Troy moved to
walk toward the door. He was cautious. He would have
to walk right past our father to exit the room. He stopped
in his tracks though when Dad reached out and roughly
grabbed my arm and shoved me toward the door.

"Get out, Jack. And close the door."

My brother's face had panic written all over it, and
I'm certain I looked worse than he did. My voice became
desperate. I fought to keep control of myself, but I
couldn't. My chest started heaving. I was gasping –
fighting for air so that I could utter words, create
sentences – reason with my father. If he could be
reasoned with. "Dad, he was on his way to change. It . . .
it was a joke, a dumb joke that's all. It was *my* idea; I
asked him to do it. I *dared* him. Please, Dad. I'm sorry,
I . . . I shouldn't have done it. I'm the oldest. It's *my*
fault. We won't be late. I'll help him get ready. Come
on Troy, I'll help . . ."

"Get out, Jack. Your brother and I need to talk." His
voice had a raspy, threatening tone.

I looked at Troy, and he looked at me with a
confidence that I knew he didn't feel. He nodded toward
the door – indicating that I should leave. "Go ahead. It's
okay."

I left the room reluctantly, and I'll never forgive myself for doing it. Troy's forgiven me. He's told me a hundred times, but I can't forgive myself. The second I was outside, the door closed tightly behind me, and I heard the click of the lock. The doors in this house were thick and heavy and my father's voice was so deadly quiet that I couldn't make out any words, but I knew he was speaking. Then, I heard him moving towards Troy.

Gram. I had to get Gram. Maybe she could stop whatever it was that was going to happen. I raced toward her room at the end of the hall but spun back around when I heard a thunderous crash followed by a shriek of pain from Troy. I flew back to the door as the voices grew louder. At the same time, Gram darted out of her door and down the hallway as fast as those marathon legs could carry her.

I pounded on the door, but it was too late. "Dad, *no*, please, no! *It's my fault!*"

"Jack, . . . honey, what's wrong? What's going on?" And then she seemed to know. She looked at my face, and she simply knew. Just then we heard my father shrieking. It was a high-pitched wail.

"Mr. Eden won't accept this! He *can't!* I've tried to make allowances for you because he's asked me to. But how can I? He's *chosen* you. But you'll never do." There was the sound of Troy's body being shoved against the wall and a groan of pain. "You just aren't going to work!"

"Chip! Chip, leave him alone! He's your own *son*! What on earth has happened to you?" Gram's voice was climbing toward the same kind of desperation that was devouring my insides. "CHIP!" She began slamming her hands against the doorframe. "I'm calling the police, Chip! I'm calling them now!" Her voice was trembling.

Again we heard the sound of contact between what I knew was Troy's body and the wall. Then, without warning, my father's voice became tearful and repentant. "*I can't make Mr. Eden understand.* You'll never work! Never." I peered through the keyhole. There was no sign of Troy, but I saw my father fall to his knees and begin to cry. He bawled like a baby, and the sobs racked his body until he collapsed the rest of the way onto the floor.

Gram had disappeared and returned with a power drill. She inserted the screwdriver attachment and proceeded to remove the entire doorknob. "Where'd that come from?" I questioned.

"My makeup bag," she said grunting as she moved into position to remove the final screw. Gram's makeup bag was a standard joke. It was more like an overnight case and contained any and all manner of oddments such as Band-Aids, tire gauges, crossword puzzles, invisible ink pens, and denture cream. It did not, however, contain makeup.

The lockset fell, and I pushed open the door to a sight of complete disarray. My father lay crumpled on the floor in much the same position as I had seen him through the keyhole. He was weeping softly and talking to himself.

Several pieces of furniture appeared to have been
jarred and jostled. Some were overturned and most,
except the bed, were out of position. Gram reached Troy
first. He was sitting on the floor and leaning against the
wall in a daze. A three-legged table, or what used to be a
three-legged table, was in pieces on either side of him.
There was a red ring around his throat where the kerchief
had been tied; I imagined my father's hands gripping it
from the underside and shoving him against the wall
repeatedly until he crumpled like a rag doll. Blood was
oozing slowly from the left side of his mouth, and his
right eye was beginning to blacken.

"Jack, help me get him up. We'll take him down to
my room." Gram's voice snapped me back to reality.
"Troy, honey . . . it's Gram. Can you hear me?" She
placed one of his arms around her shoulder just as I got
around to the other side of him and hoisted him up so that
he could place his weight between us.

"You were right, Jack," his words were slurred, but I
could make them out. "It wasn't a good idea."

By the time Gram and I got Troy onto her bed and
quieted down, my father was nowhere to be found. My
bedroom, still a complete shambles, was totally empty.
Finally, Gram decided to confront Dad, and I insisted on
going with her. She knocked on the door to his room
with strength. No answer. We entered and found
nothing. No evidence that he had even returned to his

room after the altercation. We began a search that ended quickly when we reached the garage; his car was gone.

"Well, Jack, we've got to contact the police. He's gone too far this time."

"But Gram, what about Mom? If we . . ."

"Sweetheart, your mother would *never* stand for this. I'll grant you she's not been herself these past few months, but she'd never stand for this and neither will I." As she picked up the phone and pressed *911*, I wondered if it would mean that I'd never see my mother again. I rushed to the kitchen and picked up the extension to listen.

"Paradise Operator. How may I service you?" The cheerful voice made me nauseous.

"Operator, I'd like the police." Gram's voice was steady.

There was a long pause. "I'm sorry, Ma'am. Could you repeat your request?"

Gram was perturbed with that. "The *police*. I want you to get me the police or give me the number, and I'll call them myself."

Another long pause. "What is your name? I'll need the name of the individual placing this call, please." The voice had lost all traces of the cheerfulness that had been so pervasive earlier.

I rounded the corner and shook my head "no" to Gram. She got the message.

"That's not important, Operator. I need the police. Now if you won't connect me, then I'll simply hang up and dial another operator who will."

"Ma'am," the voice returned to its original pleasant tone, "we have no police. This is *Paradise*."

At that moment, the phone connection was abruptly severed.

Chapter Eight

Despite our best efforts, phone service was not an option for the rest of the day. We had no transportation, nor did we know where to go even if we could leave. Gram decided we'd best stay put, so we returned to her room to check on Troy and decide what to do. He was feeling better – you can always tell because he starts "popping off" if he is.

"So where's dear ol' Dad – off beating up some other kids in the neighborhood?" He grinned up at us from the bed. He was amazing. Even with a black eye and a swollen lip, his sharp tongue was still at work.

Gram brushed the hair back from his eyes. "Troy, listen to me. I need you to be careful . . ."

"Oh, Gram, I'm careful. Don't worry, I'm SUPER-BOY! I'm indestructible, I'm . . ."

"Sweetheart, I'm quite aware of all that. But you have to stop being Superboy for a while." Her voice returned to that broken whisper we'd heard for the first time just a day ago when she was saying good-bye to Grampa in the apartment. "Please, Troy. I need you to promise me that you'll not make any waves with your father until we can figure out what's going on here."

As I said earlier, our grandmother was not given to
displays of vulnerability. I knew Troy would do as she
asked. He took her hand gently in his, looked solemnly
into her eyes and, in his best impression of a leading man,
said, "Anything for you, Baby. Anything for you." We
all cracked up laughing.

It was agreed that the next day Troy and I would be
dressed and ready on time. Gram thought it best that no
one mention yesterday morning's incident, and she felt
certain that my father wouldn't. While we registered and
began our first day at the school, she intended to head into
town and begin checking things out. "I watched Angela
Lansbury on that T.V. detective show of hers for four
years. I know a thing or two about detective work," she
told us with a wry smile.

The events of the following morning played out much
as we had anticipated. My father made no mention of the
previous morning's events as we ate breakfast together.
Again, clothes were laid out for Troy and me during the
night. It bothered me that someone, I assumed my father,
was entering our rooms while we slept, but there was
nothing I could do about it. I didn't think bringing it up
was a good idea.

"Well," he said cheerily, "you're all in for a real treat
today. Mother, you'll be able to 'shop 'til you drop' in
the finest stores around, and boys – you are going to love
The Garden School!"

Gram set the tone for us to play along just as we'd
agreed during our planning meeting. "I'm sure it will be

wonderful, Chip. I can hardly wait. How about you, boys?"

I chimed in right away, "Yeah, I'm psyched! Dad, didn't you say they had a lot of advanced technology at this school?"

"The best. The absolute finest of everything!" He was quite pleased with the way this conversation was developing.

"I bet they have some great coaches and sports teams, too – huh, Dad?" Bless Troy's heart. He even threw in an eager beaver grin. He shoved it out, and Dad shoveled it up.

"As a matter of fact, the sports program is unparalleled, Troy. But there's always room for another champion!" He gave Troy's arm a playful punch.

It was all I could do to stay silent and watch the bogus scenario playing out before me. How could my father swallow this? Surely he realized how phony it all was. It made me nervous that he seemed to accept, so easily, that all of a sudden we were thrilled to be here – especially after yesterday morning's fiasco. Perhaps he thought he had intimidated us to the point that we were going to embrace Paradise out of fear. In my case, at least, he might have been right.

Our journey to The Garden School was uneventful. My father celebrated the impressive features of the school from the moment we left the driveway, and Troy and I fed him enough questions to keep him delightfully content until we arrived. The school, as with all of the buildings we had seen in the village, was exceptionally beautiful, and the grounds were, of course, immaculate. It's funny. When you're constantly surrounded by beauty, you cease to appreciate it rather quickly.

After all my father's excitement about our attending The Garden School, I was shocked when he pulled up and said, "Okay, guys, hop out. Up the stairs and the office is the first door on your right."

"You mean you're not going with us?" I was stunned. It wasn't that I didn't think we could manage on our own; I had just never dreamed that he wouldn't insist on delivering us in person. That *is* how it felt – like we were being delivered.

"You boys don't need the old man tagging along on your first big day. Besides, your grandmother is waiting for me to come back and take her into town. I'll be checking up on you, though; don't worry!"

"That's a comfort." Troy just couldn't help himself. I nudged him in the ribs.

"Okay, no problem. See you after school, Dad. You picking us up here?"

"Right. Behave yourselves, boys. Remember, first impressions are everything." As he drove off, I wondered why he hadn't taken Gram with us in the first place. Probably the stores wouldn't have been open this early. I was becoming overly suspicious which, at the time, I thought was unhealthy. Hindsight, however, offers a unique vantage point.

Before we even entered the building, I prepared myself for at least an hour of filling out forms and waiting on secretaries who had "just stepped out of the office for a minute," but it wasn't like that at all. We had no sooner walked into the office, than we had everyone's full attention. And I do mean their *full* attention. They actually stopped working – all of them – and stared at us. It was a very awkward moment for me. Troy, of course, has never known an awkward moment. He stepped forward immediately and flashed those pearly whites. "I suppose you're all wondering why I've called you here," he said in a business-like voice. No one laughed. It wasn't that they seemed offended. It was more like they didn't understand that it was supposed to be funny. Finally, one woman broke the silence and stepped up toward the counter.

"You must be the boys Mr. Eden told us about – Jack and Troy, is that right? He could hardly wait for you to get here. He's been talking about your arrival for months. Welcome! It is such a privilege to have you here at The Garden School."

I wondered if she was going to come up for air. "Yeah, that's us, Jack and Troy. So do we need to fill out anything or . . ."

She interrupted, "No. Everything is in order. You are to report directly to class. I'll send for someone to take you."

We sat down, and Troy grabbed a brochure off of the table to occupy himself. Troy gets very uneasy with "down time." I, on the other hand, enjoy the chance to sit and let my mind wander. Right now, it was wandering back to the entrance gate of Paradise and to Jori, the girl who had given my life a new sense of purpose. I began to wonder if she went to this school. Perhaps, by some bizarre stroke of luck, she would be the student to escort us to our classes. She could escort me just about anywhere – I'd already made my mind up about that.

Then, I remembered my father's comment about her. He had said that she *didn't belong in Paradise*. What kind of a remark was that? What did it mean? Did it mean that she *did* live here, but that he felt she shouldn't? Or did it mean that she *didn't* live here, and that he was pleased? I was just about to bring the matter up to Troy for discussion when a lovely girl entered the office. He was on his feet instantly.

"Excuse me, Miss, but I'm new here." He threw her the classic grin and raised one eyebrow. "I don't suppose *you* could be troubled to show me to my classroom?"

His charm was clearly wasted. She stared at him blankly. "My name is Sylvia. I deliver the attendance." She gave some papers to the woman at the counter, then turned and walked out of the office.

"She's a regular party animal, huh?" His pride was clearly hurt.

"You probably just made her nervous," I said. I didn't really think that was it, but it wasn't going to kill me to stroke his ego a bit. I was still feeling an acute sense of guilt over what had happened to him yesterday morning.

Eventually, our guides came – both boys, much to Troy's chagrin – and took us to our classes. The day moved along rather quickly, and I didn't see Troy until lunch. We sat together and compared notes. We agreed on two key things. First, the teachers were incredibly knowledgeable and second, the students were equally disciplined and intelligent. No one cut up in class. Everyone's homework was completed. No one was even tardy! Troy had an additional concern.

"These girls are the pits! Not one of them has responded to my cheesy pick-up lines all morning long. Jack, I even used some of the top 10 from my *All-Time-Best Cheesy Pick-Up Lines Manual,* and I usually save those for dire emergencies!"

"Lighten up, Troy. Not *every* girl is going to be turned on by those lines of yours. Give it some time. I will say this; we're going to have to burn the midnight oil to keep up with these kids. They're smart – all of them!"

"Yeah, but they aren't any fun!" Troy complained. "I'd like to see a little spontaneity. Everyone's so stiff. I need to liven this place up a little!"

"Remember, Troy. You *promised* Gram. Let's just take it easy for a while." Just then, a gorgeous blonde came walking right past us and seated herself directly behind Troy. They were back to back. He winked at me.

"Watch this," he said with what he calls confidence, and I call arrogance. He swung his legs over the bench of our table, stood up, hooked his thumbs into his pockets and sauntered up to her table. Next, he placed his right foot on the bench she was sitting on and leaned towards her, resting his weight on his knee in a very casual pose. He raised an eyebrow playfully. My brother's modesty is overwhelming at times. Actually, most of the time. Then, he fired that grin of his and unloaded what I knew was one of his all time best lines. "Some girls say I make them go weak in the knees. What do you say?"

Once again, however, his charm was headed for a crash landing. The girl looked directly into his eyes and said, quite evenly, "I fail to comprehend why a female's knees would fail to sustain her body weight simply because she looked at you."

I nearly blew grape drink right out of my nose. Poor Troy. He sat back down looking completely baffled.

All of a sudden, we heard the clicking sound that serves as the harbinger to the public address system. An announcement was about to be made. And then, it came. *"Troy Barrett, report to Mr. Eden's office immediately. Troy Barrett, report to Mr. Eden's office immediately."* The room froze. All of the sounds of clanging silverware, people talking, and machines dispensing drinks seemed to stop in unison. The blond girl scooted down on the bench, almost imperceptibly, farther away from Troy. Everyone was looking at us. *Everyone.* There was a long pause and when the rest of the students returned to whatever had occupied them prior to the announcement, it seemed as though they were even more focused than before. It was as if they needed to refrain from looking in our direction again.   All at once, it seemed, we were outcasts. *Lepers.*

Chapter Nine

What went on in Mr. Eden's office is second-hand information. In other words, I only know as much as Troy told me. The strangest thing was that Mr. Eden was never physically in the room. The way Troy explained it, he had first reported to the main office where we'd checked in earlier in the day. The woman who had waited on us the first time escorted him with great haste through several sets of doors and down a long hallway that eventually led to an elevator. Inside the elevator was an older female attendant who, Troy claimed, would have scored a negative three on a personality scale.

"I'm telling you, Jack, that lady hasn't smiled since *Lincoln* was in office. And believe me, one look at her would convince you she was around back then. Do you know she didn't even smile when I started in with my limericks? I did Gram's favorite – you know, the *racy* one – there once was a lady named Hilda, who went for a walk with a builda' . . ."

"Troy, spare me. I've heard that one a dozen times. Will you get to what happened? You were in the elevator and . . ." I let the sentence hang there so he would take up the story again, and it worked. Troy loves being the center of attention.

"and . . . we went *down*."

"Well, thanks so much for that incredibly thorough and informative piece of information. Care to *expand* on that a little? Down to *where*?" He grinned. This was a game to him, and I was going to have to hear the story his way. He would keep me in suspense as long as possible. There are days when I could do without a little brother. But not most days.

"Did I mention the elevator was really funky? It was all decked out in fancy wood and brass and had mirrors on the top." When I did not respond, he began to focus the story. "Anyway, we went way down deep into the ground. I'm talking *way down deep*. It was wild."

I couldn't help but appreciate the differences between Troy and me as I listened to him describing his experience. I would have been completely panicked and suspicious from the onset and remained alert for danger at the turn of every corner. The hair on the back of my neck rose from simply listening to him tell the story; yet, for him, it might as well have been a carnival ride. I'm surprised he didn't ask the lady in the elevator for some cotton candy. Come to think of it, I believe he mentioned that he did.

After the elevator ride, Troy was told to depart and to go directly into Mr. Eden's "visitation office." He said the door opened by itself before he could touch it, and the lights began to come up slowly as he entered the room. He sat down and faced a huge mahogany desk with an impressive-looking but empty leather desk chair behind it.

A large computer monitor sat on the desk, but it was facing Troy's seat rather than the empty chair behind the desk. Within a moment, he said, an image appeared on the screen. Troy's description of the image sounded like the man I had seen photographing him at the wrestling meet – same black trench coat and hat.

"The weird thing," said Troy, "was that I couldn't see his face clearly. The image was distorted on the screen. I couldn't pick the guy out in a crowd if my life depended on it."

"What did his voice sound like? What did he say? Why did he call you to his office?" I was shooting questions at him much faster than he could respond.

"I don't know. His voice was quiet. It didn't sound normal. Maybe it was being filtered through a computer or something. He kept talking about all my achievements and how he hoped I would apply myself at the school. Said he'd been planning my arrival for a long time. Then, he made some really bizarre comment about my *potential for perfection* being hampered by my impulsivity and rebelliousness. Sounded like he'd been talking to Dad too much."

"What did you say?" The whole event was fascinating to me, and I had a thousand questions.

"I dunno. I said something like, 'Yeah, well impulsivity and rebelliousness go where I go. We're a package deal. But I know some really great limericks!'"

"Oh great, Troy. You sure know how to win friends and influence people. What'd he say then?"

"It looked like he kind of grinned – I'm not sure. It was hard to make out his features on the screen. Then, he told me he was finished with me for the moment and that I should leave."

"What did he mean 'finished with you *for the moment*'?"

"How should I know? The screen went dark, and the lights began to dim in the room. The door opened automatically, and when I walked into the corridor old Cora – that's what her name tag said – was waiting to give me my ride to the top."

At that moment our conversation was ended by necessity as my father's car pulled up to the front of the school. He was like a kid in a candy shop. He wanted every detail of the day, and we delivered it with enough "gee wows!" and "oh boys!" to satisfy him. We had no opportunity to talk with Gram before dinner, but she continued the charade by praising the town's shopping district and describing a few of her purchases. At the end of the meal, my father announced that he had some business to attend to and that he needed to go out for a while. Troy and I offered to clean up the supper dishes, and Gram said she needed to get to bed early. She departed for her room – at least that's the impression she gave my father.

As soon as he was gone, the kitchen "clean up" was abandoned, and the three of us met in the living room to discuss the day's events. Gram listened intently to our stories of the incredibly intelligent and well-behaved students at The Garden School. She was, of course, quite disturbed about Troy's conversation with Mr. Eden.

"Troy, I don't think you should be going down to that man's office alone anymore. It's too detached from the rest of the building. What's he doing with an office that far underground? The whole thing just isn't right. Jack, don't let your brother go down to that office alone again. Promise me." Her voice was back to its usual level of strong commanding authority.

"I promise," I said with determination.

"What a bunch of worry-warts! You two give a whole new meaning to the word *paranoid*." Troy sprung into a cartwheel that quickly transformed into a backflip. He landed in perfect form directly behind Gram who was seated quite serenely on the sofa. He placed his chin on the edge of her shoulder and eyed her shopping bags which were still lying on the floor near the foyer. "Anything in those bags a young pup like me might find interesting?" He placed his hands on her shoulders and began giving her a gentle massage which was how we always used to get rides on her motorcycle when we were younger. Now, he was simply trying to steer the discussion away from Mr. Eden and The Garden School. I looked at Gram to see if she was going to allow him to divert the flow of conversation. She tilted her head at me, and, with a look of playful exasperation, threw up her hands and shrugged.

"Oh, I believe a pair of those fancy-shmancy sunglasses you were eyeing last summer might have found their way into one of my shopping bags, handsome." She hopped over to her bags and began to deliver the prizes. "And Jack, I picked up a college dictionary for you!"

Great. Troy gets *studglasses*, and I get a dictionary. Is there any justice in life?

"And, of course, a pair of sunglasses as well!" I felt her putting them over my head from behind. So, Gram hadn't forgotten me after all. I was a little ashamed of myself.

"Whoa! What about *my* dictionary?" Troy began imitating some serious emotional pain. "Aren't you afraid of damaging my sensitive self-esteem?"

"Troy Barrett, the last dictionary I got you was used as a skateboard ramp and a free weight but never to look up any words! Not to mention the time I found you playing baseball and using it . . ."

"Gram, we *needed* a home plate!" Troy was being overly dramatic as usual. For a moment, the seriousness of the situation in Paradise melted away, and I enjoyed listening to them spar with one another.

"You didn't need to use the dictionary your grandmother gave you on your tenth birthday as a home plate! I had a million things in my make-up bag you could have used!"

"How was I to know?" Troy questioned.

"You had only to ask," she countered.

Soon they were "play wrestling," and I laughed at them until someone grabbed my pant leg, and I was

pulled into the huddle.   Then, it became a fight for
survival of the fittest. As usual, Gram won.

"Now listen, boys," she said as we began climbing
back onto the furniture. "I need to talk to you about
something a bit more serious." All traces of the playful
scene from moments ago vanished. We were all ears. "I
did some checking when I was in town today. I tried to
find a realty office and had absolutely no success. Your
father mentioned before the move that Mr. Eden required
all of his employees living in Paradise to sign an
agreement that they would resell their homes to him at
fair market value if and when they decided to leave the
village. Well, according to your father, Mr. Eden sells the
homes to the employees at remarkably low prices. So, if
someone wanted to make some good money . . ."

"I get it!" I jumped in. "An employee could buy the
house from Mr. Eden at the fantastic low price, then
decide to leave Paradise and resell it to him at the *fair
market price* – which would obviously be much higher!"

"Now nobody with any scruples would do such a
thing, but as you know, boys, the world is full of
unscrupulous people. I was certain that some of Mr.
Eden's employees had, over the years, made a profit off
of this arrangement."

"What kind of pea-brain sets things up like that?"
said Troy. "How can this guy be so successful by doing
something so stupid? Why would anyone do that?"

"That's what I was trying to find out. And here's the
disturbing part, boys. When I couldn't find a realty

office, I began asking people on the street to help me, but no one seemed to have any knowledge of where I might find one; furthermore, every person I stopped looked at me as though my question was ridiculous. One woman seemed almost offended that I had asked. She asked if I understood that this was Paradise. When I said that yes, I was quite aware of that, she asked me why I thought anyone would ever want to leave Paradise. Then, she walked off in a huff before I could respond. Finally, I went to the only governmental office I could find. This one building apparently houses all documentation of a legislative nature. When I began inquiring about property sold, the young lady waiting on me was most evasive. She told me that Mr. Eden sells all the property in Paradise. When I asked about people reselling their homes back to him, she was clearly astounded.

"'Ma'am,' she said to me, 'nothing like that has ever happened here.'"

"Well, certainly it has," I told her. "People leave the company, people retire, people move away. Certainly they sell their homes before they leave."

Boys, this young woman looked at me so innocently that it was clear what I was suggesting was simply beyond her ability to comprehend. And then she said, very calmly, "*Leave?* What do you mean *leave?* This is Paradise. No one leaves here. *Ever.*"

It took a minute for me to even figure out how I wanted to respond to this new piece of information. Even Troy didn't seem to have a comment on the tip of his tongue. His eyes were grave. The seriousness of what Gram had told us was obviously not lost on him.   I started to suggest that maybe the lady was simply new to the job or that she had been pulled from another department this afternoon, when the front door opened quite suddenly.

My father walked into the room as if he were Grand Marshal of a parade. "Hey everyone!" He looked so pleased he was ready to burst. "Mom's home!"

"MOM!" Troy and I echoed in unison and jumped to our feet. We raced toward the foyer, but I stopped short as she entered the house.

The woman before us looked rested and seemed completely poised. There was an air of confidence about her. Every detail of her appearance was flawless. There was only one problem. *She wasn't our mother*.

Chapter Ten

It's very difficult to describe the kind of anxiety and uncertainty that washed over me as my gaze met that of the woman being presented as my mother. For all intents and purposes, she did *appear* to be my mother. But she wasn't. I knew it, yet I had no reason – no logical support for my position. She held Troy in a loving embrace and then cocked an eyebrow at me questioningly – a familiar gesture which suddenly, for no good reason, seemed totally wrong.

"Jack . . ." she said it as though she was fishing for a verbal response from me. "Sweetheart, aren't you glad to see me? I left the retreat early because I missed you boys so much."

It seemed the only choice I had was to play the part of the welcoming son. Either that, or accuse this woman of being an impostor with no evidence whatsoever to substantiate my claim. "Uhhh . . . yeah, Mom, sure." I moved to meet her with a quick embrace as Troy stepped back. The hug was awkward. She felt stiff, but the smell of her favorite perfume eased my discomfort somewhat.

"Susan, sweetheart, we've all missed you so." Gram took her turn. They embraced, and Gram gave her an affectionate kiss on the cheek. My mother had always adored Gram – partially because she lost her own mother when she was a junior in college, but also because Gram had always treated her as if she were her own daughter.

"Katy, I've missed you, too. You've been such a doll to take care of Chip and the boys while I was away."

I was trying to get a look from either Gram or Troy that would tell me if they had noticed anything peculiar, but both of them seemed completely enamored with this fraud. I couldn't get a read on the situation and was wondering if I'd have to spend the majority of the evening trying to convince them that this woman was not who she appeared to be when my father's voice interrupted my thoughts.

"Well, that's enough excitement for one evening. Your mother needs to get some rest, boys. She's had a long trip today." He took her by the arm. "Let's go on up, Susan." They had ascended only the first few stairs when she stopped, turned to pull something out of a small travel bag, and held it out for our inspection. It was her first big mistake.

"Oh, boys," she said as she turned the object in her hand so that the light danced off its shiny edges, "we were never really apart. Right?" She smiled then, placed the object back into her bag, and they proceeded up to their room.

I felt the color drain from my face. With fingers dipped in scarlet polish, she had showcased a brass picture frame – two hearts joined in the middle. Troy and I were pictured as always. It was exactly the same as the day we gave it to her. The glass was in perfect condition. So how was it that I had the same pictures . . . the same frame – but with broken glass – hidden in my nightstand upstairs? Troy stumbled backwards slightly, and Gram steadied him. None of us spoke as Dad and "Mom" climbed the stairs.

Thankfully, the picture incident was all it took to convince Gram and Troy that something was very wrong with the woman claiming to be my "mother." They were not, however, totally willing to concede that she was an impostor. Rather than argue until the wee hours of the night, Gram thought it best that we all get a good night's rest. There would be plenty of opportunities for us to observe "Mom" in the days ahead, she pointed out, and at this point we had nowhere to turn for help anyway. Troy and I trudged reluctantly upstairs while Gram returned to the kitchen to tidy up.

It was half past three; I remember because I sat straight up in bed, and my digital alarm clock was staring me in the face from across the room. The nightmare had been a real doozy. My brother had been back in Mr. Eden's office. He was locked inside, and the room was filling up with some kind of poisonous gas. I was on the other side of the door, but I couldn't get to him. And Mr. Eden's shadowy face was on the computer screen laughing. His laugh grew louder and more ominous as my brother began to suffocate from the gas. Troy was crying out to me, but I had no way to help him!

Now that I was awake and aware of my surroundings, I could feel the sweat running down my arms and legs in tiny rivulets. I jumped out of bed and made my way to Troy's room. Since his door was half-open, I stepped quietly inside. My eyes had adjusted to the darkness so there was no need for a light. As soon as I saw that he was okay, I'd head back to bed. My eyes scanned the bed. Nothing. All of a sudden I could hear the pulsing of my heart in my ears. *Troy wasn't in the room.* Fighting a growing sense of panic, I turned on his closet light and began to inspect the room. His bed covers were twisted into an abominable mess – proof that he had, indeed, been sleeping in this bed. I knelt to look under the bed, half certain that his hand would shoot out and grab me – in which case he would die a thousand deaths by the time I was finished with him. No such luck, but I did find an old rag. It looked like a remnant from a cheap piece of cloth. I didn't recognize it, but I did notice that it had a dampness to it. I held it up to my nose, took a deep whiff, and grabbed the bedframe as the room began to spin. Whatever was on that rag nearly knocked me right off my feet!

I waited a moment for my head to clear and then considered my options, which at the moment seemed rather sparse. It would serve no purpose to wake anyone when I hadn't even checked the house to see if Troy was around. Hunting for him alone on the first two floors would be only slightly creepy, but I knew that the basement would need to be checked, too. I had never been to the basement of this house. In fact, I had rarely been to the basement in our old house; something about the whole "underground" thing really bothers me. Still, I set off on my quest with as stout a heart as I could muster.

My search of the first two floors turned up nothing. No great surprise. That rag had *foul play* written all over it. I had already convinced myself that someone had knocked Troy out and taken him – but the where and why were a mystery. I opened the basement door and switched on the light. Then I began my descent. Why couldn't this fancy house have a finished basement? Then, at least, going down under the ground would seem a little more hospitable. As I explored the basement from one end to the other, the cool concrete seemed to work its way through the soles of my bare feet and send a chill all the way up my spine. While my search for Troy was fruitless, I did make a rather interesting discovery. Though no rooms had been framed in the basement, I found what appeared to be a finished closet at the farthest end of the house. The closet had a heavy six-panel door on brass hinges with a fancy curved knob. It was open and inside, on the rear wall, there were two hooks – the smaller positioned slightly above the larger one. Next to the closet was another door which appeared to be locked although I could find no locking mechanism. I gave up fairly quickly when the "mystery" door wouldn't open. Basements and mystery doors are not, in my opinion, a good combination.

I returned quickly to the first floor and checked the outside doors for any sign of forced entry. Everything seemed in perfect order. If someone had kidnapped my brother, he or she obviously knew how to get in and out of the house without creating a disturbance. *Kidnapped.* There. I had finally said the word in my mind, but I still couldn't quite grasp it. What other explanation could there be? And yet, if Troy had been kidnapped, I knew it was not for a ransom. There was some other reason, and I hated to think what it could be. Heading for Gram's room as quickly and quietly as possible, I froze in my tracks when I saw the doorknob to my parents' room turning slowly. Then I stood there, dumbstruck, as I heard the soft click of the latch from behind their door. A noise from Troy's room spurred me to action. I raced into his room, and there he was – lying on his bed as if nothing had happened. I closed the door and tried to wake him.

"*Troy, Troy, wake up.*" I shook him but couldn't get much of a response. "Troy, are you all right? Where have you been? Did someone hurt you? I've been looking everywhere for you. Troy, what's going on?" My brother has always been incredibly hard to wake, so it was hard to tell for sure if he was more "out of it" than usual. I shook him again and finally he began to show signs of life. "Troy, wake up. Where have you been?"

"Huh . . . huh . . . Jack? What's up, man? What are you doin' here? What time is it anyway?"

"Troy, you haven't been in your room! Where have you been?" He looked me in the eyes finally, but I could tell he was not altogether with me.

"What are you talking about? I've been right here in my bed. Asleep. It's what most of us do at night! Who are you, my nanny?" He giggled to himself as if he were still half asleep.

I shook him harder. "Troy, this is serious. You weren't in this room thirty minutes ago. And this rag I found . . . it . . ." I couldn't believe my eyes. The rag was gone. I had left it lying on the floor – right where I had found it. And now, it was nowhere in sight. I began searching for it – crawling completely underneath the bed but to no avail. By the time I had completed my inspection, Troy had lapsed back into his semi-comatose state. There seemed no point in trying to wake him again. What was I going to do, other than frighten him? It seemed clear that he had no knowledge of ever having been outside his room. Still, I was not about to leave him alone. I wedged a chair underneath his doorknob, sat down on the Oriental rug my father had insisted on having in every bedroom for as far back as I could remember, and leaned my weary body against the wall.

I could feel my eyes beginning to close as I surveyed the room again; however, when I reached the far left corner I saw something that jolted me wide awake. I rose and walked across the room for a closer inspection of the items that I knew had not been in the room during my earlier visit that night. Troy's school clothes, crisp and clean as usual, had been laid out on the antique sofa and ottoman just as they had been the previous two nights. What was much more disturbing, though, was the fact that next to his uniform was a second one. *Mine.* Someone wanted me to know that my whereabouts during the evening hadn't been as secretive as I had hoped. Did he . . . or she . . . or could it be *they*, realize that I had found the rag, too? Was it also common knowledge that I was aware that someone had removed my brother from his room? Basically, I was asking myself – did "they" know that *I* knew? I rubbed my tired eyes and looked at my uniform lying next to Troy's. Yes, they knew all right. The question was, what were they going to do about it?

Chapter Eleven

Sleep, sound sleep, never came to me that night, and I returned to my room a few minutes before Troy's alarm clock sounded. I decided to allow the morning to play out and see if there was any indication of the previous night's events from the breakfast crowd.

"Good morning, Jack, dear. What would you like for breakfast?"

I stood just inside the kitchen door gawking at "Mom." I'm sure the look on my face identified me as a total moron, but I couldn't help it. Her hair was extravagantly arranged in large curls, and her face was fully made up. She wore an emerald green dress that brought out the green in her eyes and accented her auburn hair quite nicely. Gold and diamond bracelets encircled her wrists and long dangling earrings caught the light so that they sparkled mercilessly. Ditch the apron and she was ready to model for *Mademoiselle*. I saw this as a bit of a problem since it was 7:00 A.M. and, to my knowledge, she had nowhere to go.

"Jack?" She questioned my silence.

"Oh. Yeah. Ummm, whatever . . . cereal is fine."

"Cereal! Don't be silly. Cereal is *not* part of a balanced breakfast. *Everyone knows that.*"

Her words sounded hollow. Like a recording on the
P.A. system at school.

"I'll make you some eggs and bacon. Sit down,
Dear."

I sat. My father, who had occupied himself with the
paper until this moment, suddenly began to eat his
morning meal. I noted the juice, milk, and toast that
accompanied the main course. It seemed that "Mom" was
interested in showcasing her talents on her first day back.

"Quite a spread your mother's provided here, Jack.
Wouldn't you say?"

"Yeah, Dad. Sure. It's terrific."

All at once Troy burst through the door. "Ta, dah!
The Garden School's most eligible bachelor arrives on the
scene. The fans go wild! The girls all cheer! The . . ."

My father's disapproving look ended Troy's morning
moment of glory. My brother immediately refocused.
You can't keep Troy down for long.

"Whoa! Check it out! Mom, what's the story? You
plannin' to turn some heads around town today?"

I knew Troy didn't believe this woman was our
mother – at least not the way she used to be – but he was
clearly more at ease with pretending than I was. We had
all agreed to accept her for the time being – but for me it
was easier said than done.

"Oh, Troy, my you are funny. I don't want to turn
heads. That might be harmful to people. I simply want to
look nice for your father. For all of you. I want the

family to be proud of me. Just as you should. Just as we all should. *Just as we all should.*"

I was accepting my breakfast plate from her when it happened – the repeated phrase and then an awkward moment when she didn't release the plate. We both had our hands on it, but she wouldn't let go. No. It wasn't that she *wouldn't* let go; it was that she *couldn't* let go. And, she had repeated herself.

My father looked up abruptly, and as he did, she released the plate. He practically leaped to her side. "Susan, I believe you're looking tired, darling. Why don't you lie down for a while? Don't worry about making another breakfast. Troy can have cereal." He began leading her out of the kitchen.

"Cereal is *not* part of a balanced breakfast. *Everyone knows that*," she said in that same monotone. He shoved her ahead of him through the door.

"What was that all about?" Troy looked at me curiously as he dumped Frosted Flakes into a cereal bowl and smothered them with honey. He loves them that way. No milk either.

"I told you something's wrong with her. Big time! Troy, did you hear her repeat herself? And my plate. She couldn't let go of it for a minute. And *he* couldn't get her out of here fast enough. The whole thing smells . . ."

"Suspicious!" Gram entered the room, and we burst into laughter. She had on one of those incredibly large pair of sunglasses – the kind that extend on either side of your face by at least four inches. They were bright pink.

She was clad in a sleek jogging suit that was a pale shade of lavender. A mint green turtleneck rounded out her attire. She was always the fashion plate, but the glasses were too much. "It's all suspicious, and today, while you boys are at school, I'm going to get to the bottom of this." The large overnight case, her makeup bag, was hoisted into a chair. She then removed the sunglasses and placed them inside as Troy leaned over in his seat to try to get a look. She closed the lid tightly. "No peeking!"

"Just once I wanna look in that thing! You gotta repack it daily. I've never seen you take the same thing out of it twice."

"Troy, you little devil, I do *no such thing*. Besides, what a woman keeps in her makeup bag is no concern of yours. Now listen, boys. I'm leaving the village today. I want to do some more checking on things. I'll be back by early evening, and I want you both to promise me that you won't do anything to cause a problem – either at school or at home – 'til I'm back. Promise?" She was looking at Troy.

"Oh, I promise, Grandmother. Certainly I do. As for my brother, Jack, I cannot say. He is a wild child. Untempered. Provocative. Recklessly indulgent and disobedient. Still, I shall do my best to . . ."

"Can it." I looked at him and grinned. I really like my little brother.

Gram gave us quick kisses and hugs and headed out the back door. We were to tell Dad that she went on a morning run and would be shopping most of the day. Her timing was great. He arrived within minutes of her departure, and the three of us headed to the car. He explained that "Mom" had overexerted herself and that she was resting.

One day at The Garden School was much like the next. Troy and I basically hung together whenever we could. The other students remained aloof. They were totally committed to their studies and completely uninterested in any discussion of a social nature. What was even more upsetting, particularly to Troy, was that the guy-girl connection didn't seem to be happening. Anywhere. For that matter there didn't seem to be a guy-guy connection – like the major studs hanging out together. Or a girl-girl connection – where they all head into the girls' bathroom to gossip. These kids weren't connected to anything.

I was heading to my math class after lunch when I started thinking about a connection *I'd* like to make. She was back at that gatehouse. Or at least she might be by the time school got out. I found Troy in the hallway and told him I was ditching the rest of the afternoon.

"No way! I'm not staying in *Happy Land* all afternoon while you go put the moves on your gatehouse girlfriend!" He was going to be difficult.

"Troy, look. We can't both go. You have to stay. When Dad comes to pick us up, tell him I'm staying after school to do research in the library. I'll be home by dinner. It's gonna take me a while to get to the gatehouse on foot. If I leave now, I'll be there by 3:30, and maybe she'll be there."

"You don't even know if she's working today. Or where she goes to school. You don't know anything about her! If you go, *I* go."

"Come on, Troy. I'd do it for you." Then, I knew how to get him. I arched my eyebrow, a sloppy job compared to his technique, but you work with what you've got, and I gave him my most persuasive grin. "She *might* have a sister." Given his record of strikeouts here, I knew this would get his attention.

"Well, well, well . . . now that *is* a charming thought!" He was beaming. "You *will* tell her, the sister that is, because she's *bound* to have one, that I am best described as a *young god*. That I'm handsomer than all get-out – remember to say it the way Gram does, Jack. Tell her I'm funny yet sentimental, intelligent but with common sense, adventurous yet . . ."

"All right, all right. I'll tell her. *If* there's a sister."

His face indicated he was going to go sour on me again.

"Which . . . I'm sure there is!" I turned and raced out of the building.

As I jogged through the streets of Paradise, I kept wondering if Jori would be at the gatehouse. If not, I decided I would talk *about* her to whoever *was* there. Surely a girl like Jori would be well known and liked by all of the gatehouse staff.

At last it was in sight. I sped up, rounded the corner, and caught my breath. She was there! I could see her through the window. My heart went into its somersault routine again. No cars were around, so I approached the small door and knocked.

She opened the door and when she saw me, the smile that lit up her face told me that I'd been on her mind these past few days. I knew then that this girl was truly something special. "Hi, Jack."

"Hi." Pause. "I thought we should . . . that is . . . I mean . . . we left kind of abruptly the other day. I wanted to apologize."

"Oh, that's okay. Your father's a very busy man. I can't imagine he has time for . . ."

"That's no excuse. I would never have been so rude. Not to *you*."

She took my hand. "Why don't you come inside?"

I didn't know where this was going, but *inside* holding her hand was definitely better than *outside* tripping over my tongue. The next hour was probably the most valuable investment of time in my entire life. Jori told me all about her family. She had terrific parents. Troy would be thrilled to hear that her sister Julie was a redhead. I asked to see a picture. She was drop-dead gorgeous and a freshman. Jori also had two younger brothers, Michael and David. She lived in Hampton Chase, the next town over and rode her bike here to work after school each day. She also worked on weekends

occasionally.   She was a major volleyball player and
loved school – except for science classes.

"So what's it like working here?" I asked her. "I
mean, what do you do?" I had noticed that not one car
had entered or left the entire time I'd been there.

"Mostly just see to it that the village remains
protected," she replied.

"Protected? What's that mean?" I was really hoping
that Jori wasn't going to turn out to be connected with
this place to any great extent.

"Come on, Jack. You of all people ought to know
how the village works. I mean your father . . ."

"Let's not talk about my father. He's not a favorite
topic of mine lately. Now tell me what you mean by
protected?"

"Well. Like this." She pulled an official looking pad
of paper over and began reading some kind of report
silently. "See this *incident report*? This was logged early
this morning. An older woman tried to leave the village.
She . . ."

The tension ran down my spine like lightning. "What
older woman? Who? When? What was she wearing?"

"Jack, what's wrong? I don't know who. It just says
that an elderly female was apprehended this morning
when she . . . Jack? What is it? Why are you staring at
that? *Do you know this woman*?"

It was sitting barely two feet from me. I could have
seen it. Would have seen it. If I hadn't been so caught up
in playing the leading man. "This overnight case," I said,

"it belongs to my grandmother. She's the woman in the report." I grabbed her shoulders. "Jori. Where is she? What happened to her? Good grief, what did she do wrong?"

"I don't know where she is, Jack. Why would she try to do such a thing? It's not as though she can just *leave* Paradise."

"Why not? Why *can't* she leave? She was going back to our old town. She was going to find some answers. Why can't she leave?" I let go of her shoulders as my stomach dropped. I knew something. Something ugly. I looked at her intently. "Jori, *I* can't leave here either. Can I?"

She backed away from me. "You . . . you didn't know? But how could you *not* know? Everyone knows." The sadness in her voice was unmistakable. It was like she was apologizing – like she should have told me.

"Jori," I pleaded with her. "Please. *What happened to my grandmother?* Don't you know anything? How did they stop her? How would *you* stop *me*? Right now. If I ran out of this gatehouse and turned left and headed . . ." I moved toward the door.

"Jack! DON'T!" She grabbed my arm – hard. "You can't go *left* out of this gatehouse. You'll be immobilized by an electric current." She looked at the floor.

"WHAT? What are you talking about? How? What *is* this place? What has he *done* to us? Immobilized? How? You go left out of this gatehouse every day when you leave here, but *I* can't?   Why don't *you* get immobilized?"

"I would," she said with a trace of bitterness. "If I tried to go *right*. I don't belong in Paradise, Jack. And you and your grandmother don't belong outside of it."

Chapter Twelve

My mind had more questions than there was time for her to answer. How did this *system* know the difference between us? Who installed it and why? Had it always been this way? If it was so secure, why a gatehouse? But the most important question had to do with Gram, who I now believed was in real danger. "Jori, are you saying that my grandmother was shocked? Electrically?"

"Yes, Jack. She was. I'm so sorry."

"Is she okay? Is she alive? What happens when this kind of thing occurs?"

"I really don't know too much. It happens rarely. Your father usually comes to take care of these kinds of situations, I think."

"My *father*. He knows about this? About my grandmother?" She could hear the tone of my voice, and it scared her. It should have.

"Jack, I . . . I can't say for sure. I wasn't here. Maybe. Maybe he knows. Probably. He probably does."

"I gotta go." I nearly ripped the gatehouse door off its hinges as I threw it open and scrambled toward home. I ran like there was no tomorrow. I just left her there. Me. The guy who was so worried about people being rude to her. I unloaded all of this and left her standing there trying to make sense of it all. I made a mental note never again to fall in love with a girl when my family was in the process of being abducted and permanently secured in a mysterious village by invisible fencing. Very bad timing.

I was making my way up the driveway with no recollection of the trip there. My only thoughts were of my grandmother. Would she be in the house? Did my father, in fact, know what had happened? If so, what would he do? It was now clear that he was beyond reason. Still, I reminded myself, it would do no good to challenge him at this point.

I opened the door, and they were all in the living room except Gram. "Mom" was seated on the sofa in a wine-colored velvet evening dress. She had Troy's hand in hers. My father stood behind her with one hand on her shoulder. His other hand was moving gently across Troy's shoulders with what was supposedly paternal affection. Troy looked up as I entered. His eyes were red, and when he saw me they welled up in tears without hesitation. "Jack. Jack, it's Gram," he said. "She fell, and I don't know . . ." He couldn't continue.

I measured my words to my father carefully. "What happened? Where was she? How did it happen?"

He delivered without a moment of hesitation. Perhaps when you deceive your family on a regular basis it becomes instinctual. "Jack, your grandmother *fell* while jogging today. It happened in the park. She's in her room, and Mr. Eden has had a doctor visit her already.

She's been given some pain medication to help her rest, and I'm afraid . . ."

"Let me guess," I said. The sarcasm was creeping into my voice despite my best efforts to control it. I didn't want him to know that I already knew the truth. "No one can see her right now. Right?"

"As a matter of fact, you're correct, Jack. No one *can* see her." He gave me a long, hard stare.

"When you've had a bad fall, no one can see you. *Everyone knows that.*" Another insightful comment from "Mom." She was sure to be a lot of fun at parties.

I walked toward my brother. "Come on Troy. Let's go upstairs. There's nothing we can do right now."

"Your brother's right, Troy. You guys go on up to your rooms. I'll keep you posted on your grandmother's condition. This is *most* unfortunate."

Most unfortunate. *Right.* My thoughts exactly. I bolted the door to Troy's room, and we went into his closet where I proceeded to tell him everything I knew about Paradise.

"That *slimeball*! We gotta do something, Jack. We can take him – the two of us together. We gotta get out of here! We're gonna get Gram and get out of here. They're nuts. What have they done to us? Why are they trying to keep us here? *How* are they keeping us here?"

"Troy, I don't know. I didn't have time to get into the details with Jori, but I have an idea. I *have* to see Gram, Troy. Now. You're going to have to keep a look out and cover for me if necessary." He agreed, and I headed for her room as quickly and quietly as possible. I don't think my father ever considered that I would disobey him and enter Gram's room. I was the good boy, and Troy was too distraught to challenge him – or so he thought.

She was very drowsy. I didn't recognize the medication, but I assumed it was some kind of drug to make her tired. Still, when she saw it was me, she tried to sit up. "Gram," I said. "Lie still. I'm here with you. I've been to the gatehouse. I know what happened. You received some kind of electric shock."

She nodded her agreement and pointed to her water glass. After a long drink she began to speak with pained effort. "Jack, go . . . go back home. Bill . . ." She was beginning to doze again.

"Gram. *Gram*, stay with me. Bill who? Bill Simpson? Grampa's friend? Gram!" I shook her.

"Yes, Simpson. Bill Simpson. Ask him . . . about the stock. *Chip's* stock. Tell him Katy needs . . . to know about your father's stock . . . Tell him . . ."

That was all she was going to be good for. I kissed her forehead. "Don't worry, Gram. I'll go see him. I'll ask him about the stock." It was difficult to imagine that I was going to leave the two of them alone in this house, but there didn't seem to be any other choice. I pulled the covers up close around my grandmother. "You're going to be okay, Gram. I'm going to make sure of it." I stole quietly back to Troy's room and charged him with seeing to Gram's safety.

"You just leave our grandmother in these capable hands," he said reassuringly. "Perhaps I've mentioned before that these hands of mine are registered as *lethal weapons* with . . ."

"T-r-o-y," I drew out his name to indicate that we had no time for funny stuff.

He rebounded immediately. "Okay. So, you said you had an idea? *Is it a plan, Jack*? What are we gonna do?"

"I'm still working on it. Give me tonight," I said with more confidence than I felt. "Just give me tonight." I left for my room with nothing on my mind but the plan, and as I lay in bed, I went over each detail again and again. It all hinged on one thing. Jori. She was the only one who could help us. The question was – would she? I remembered the look in her eyes when she saw me at the gatehouse door today. Yes, I smiled. She would.

I looked at the clock. It was 3:00 A.M., and I hadn't slept a wink. I decided to wake Troy and fill him in now; besides, we would need to do some planning together to pull this thing off. I had just entered the hallway when I saw the door to his room closing slowly. I rushed down the hall, worried that his "night visitor" was back, and as I peered cautiously through the crack in the door, I drew in a breath so fast I was certain it was audible. He was wearing the familiar black trench coat and hat. *Mr. Eden was in the house*!

My first thought was to jump into the room and expose him, and yet I was learning to be cautious. Mr. Eden and my father clearly had all of the power in

Paradise. Troy was not in clear danger as far as I knew. Perhaps it would be more advantageous for both of us if I didn't move too hastily. I decided to watch and listen for the moment.

Mr. Eden quickly drew a cloth and bottle from his coat. He dumped some of the liquid from the bottle onto the cloth and pressed it quickly over Troy's nose and mouth. "Time for you to sleep a little more soundly, Troy." His voice was little more than a whisper. It sounded dark. *Evil.*

He grabbed my brother roughly, placed him in a fireman's carry, and moved toward the door. I jumped out of the way and hid in the bathroom doorway long enough to see him move toward the stairs with Troy. Then, I remained at the top and watched – expecting him to head for the front door, but he didn't. He circled around the corner and opened the door to *the basement*!

I rocketed down the main staircase and headed stealthily toward the basement. I took those stairs much more cautiously. First, because I didn't know how far ahead Mr. Eden was and I couldn't risk him hearing me, and second, because I *hate* going underground! By the time I got down there and made my way to the two doors, there was no sign of Mr. Eden and Troy. The closet, which was open, had Mr. Eden's black trench coat on one hook and his hat on the smaller hook up above. I tried the other door, but it was locked as it had been before.

Instantaneously, I was riddled with guilt. What was happening to Troy? Could I have stopped it? No. No, I couldn't. I would easily have been overpowered if I'd tried. It seemed the only thing I could do for the moment was either pound on this door and throw a fit, which didn't seem like a terribly good plan, or wait for Troy's return. I looked into the closet again. Mr. Eden's coat. I began to search it as quickly as possible reminding myself that if this were a slasher movie I would be discovered searching the coat by Mr. Eden himself, and he would likely cut me open with an ax.

Fortunately, I remained in one piece and came away from my search with one clue. A *receipt* from Wakefield Monument Company. The name sounded vaguely familiar, though at the time I couldn't place it. Still, I decided to hang onto the receipt since it was the only scrap of information I had on Mr. Eden. Just then, I heard noises coming from behind the secret door. It sounded as though someone was unfastening several locking mechanisms. I returned to the base of the stairs and ascended quickly. In fact, I went all the way up and into Troy's room where I hid in the closet. Now that I was finally *facing* Mr. Eden, instead of looking at him from behind, I was determined to memorize every feature of his face. In fact, I pictured it on a WANTED poster! He did return to the room; however, his face remained shielded from view. The darkness of the room in combination with his hat, which was pulled down low, and his coat collar, which was turned up all around his face, prevented me from distinguishing any specific characteristics. I did, however, notice something familiar slung over his right arm. He replaced Troy just as he had found him and then lifted the clothes hanger into view. He walked cautiously over to the sofa and ottoman and laid out Troy's school clothes for the next morning – never uttering a sound. Then, he left the room in great haste.

My brother never stirred. He didn't appear to be hurt, but obviously he had been taken from the room for a reason. I was caught between wanting to follow Mr. Eden on his exit from the house and needing to confirm that Troy was all right. After all, I had basically allowed him to be temporarily abducted by someone I certainly didn't trust. I rushed to the bed – Mr. Eden would have to wait. I didn't even worry about waking Troy; I basically inspected what I could see of him. There was no evidence of bruising or any kind of abuse. His wrists and ankles did not appear to have been tied with anything. There was nothing to indicate that his clothing had been removed. There were no red marks around his face that might indicate Mr. Eden had hooked him up to some kind of machine. I didn't really know what I was looking for, but I knew my brother was being taken out of this room for something, and it wasn't for anything good!

Based on my last experience with Troy and his night visitor, I saw no point in trying to wake him now. It was also pointless to search for Mr. Eden. I had been with Troy for so long that I was sure the proprietor of Paradise was long gone from the house. I left for my room, and when I arrived I found my clothes for The Garden School

– perfectly pressed and ready for me. I looked to my bed and sighed with relief. Lady luck had smiled on me. I had left the covers in such a state of disarray that, in the dark, it appeared that I was in bed. Thank goodness. If it had been clear that I was not in my room, what would Mr. Eden have done?

The next day Troy and I ditched our morning classes. He agreed to return to school for the afternoon and tell them I was sick. Eventually, we would get caught, but we hoped we wouldn't be around long enough for that to happen. Troy agreed to keep a watchful eye on Gram. Then, I told him about what had happened to him the night before. My eyes became misty as I heard myself telling my brother that I stood by and watched while someone took him away for God knows what purpose. He punched me and grinned.

"Aaaah! Ya big cry baby. I'm fine. They're probably photographing this face for some teen girl pin-up calendar, and they don't want to split the profits with me!"

I suggested he pull an "all-nighter" so that he could guard against another one of Mr. Eden's visits. If our plan worked, I would be back tomorrow, and we would be out of here.

I knocked on the door of the gatehouse, and there she was. Next, came the smile. I knew she would help me. I quickly filled Jori in on the entire story. She might as well know about her potential in-laws right up front.

Now, for the big question. Did she know how to shut down the electrical current surrounding the village? Yes. Would she do it – for me? Just for a moment? Long enough for me to get through? Yes. Would I definitely be safe in trying this? She had no idea.

"Jori," I took her hand. "I want you to flip the power switch off for a split second. Nothing more. If my father finds out that you're doing this on purpose . . . he just can't. He *mustn't* know that you're involved in this." I pulled her toward me rather awkwardly and kissed her. I was pleased to find, throughout the duration of this kiss, that I was not the only one doing the kissing. Now if I could just stay alive, there would be romance to return to – a very motivating factor for young heroes!

I watched her walk over to an orange lever on the wall. "This is it, Jack. I'll only have it off for a minute. Go outside the door and watch for me to pull down on the lever. Good luck!" She reached up and tried to pull it down. At first it wouldn't budge, but then she gripped it with both hands, and I saw it coming down. I barreled forward without hesitation.

I was unprepared for the tremendous jolt of electricity that sent a searing pain coursing through my body a moment later. I screamed in agony.

Chapter Thirteen

Soft hands were gently caressing the sides of my face; I opened my eyes to a blurry vision that slowly came into focus. I was staring into the most beautiful eyes in the world, but at the moment they held a look of genuine concern. I realized, all at once, that my head was resting in Jori's lap. Then, I remembered the electric shock. Jori had apparently come to my rescue. "Great," I chided myself, "my girlfriend plays the heroine while I get knocked on my butt. It never happens this way in the movies," I thought.

"Jack, are you all right?" She helped me sit up.

"Yeah." I moved my arms and pulled my legs up toward my chest. It was nice to see they could still move. "What happened? I thought you were shutting off the power?"

"I was. I mean, I did. That lever must not be used much. It came down very slowly. I had to keep pulling at it to get it all the way down. You must have started running as soon as you saw it moving, huh?"

"Yep." I sighed – blowing air up the front of my face so that my hair lifted up off my forehead for a minute. "Troy's usually the impulsive one. I can't believe I didn't wait to make sure it was all the way down!" I considered

my location for a moment. "Hey! I'm out! I made it!"
So maybe the shock was worth it after all. I was free
from the village, and the extra attention from Jori was
more than making up for the price I'd paid.

"Just be glad that lever was already partially down
when you went through," she said. "Imagine if you'd
gotten the full shock!" As soon as she said it, she
regretted it. I could read it on her face. We both had the
same thought. *My grandmother had taken the full shock.*

Without warning we both became uncomfortable.
She stepped back. I think that somehow she was feeling
responsible for what happened, which didn't make any
sense, or maybe she was just angry with herself for
reminding me of Gram.

She stared at the ground awkwardly. "I better get back
to the gatehouse, Jack . . . be careful."

"Yeah. You, too." I watched her walk away in
silence, and then, as fate would have it, an important
thought struck me. I had forgotten to make arrangements
with her to reenter the village. Feeling like the supreme
idiot, I shouted to her just as the gatehouse door was
closing. "Jori, wait!" She came running back.

"Yes?" Her eyes sparkled with excitement and
anticipation.

"I forgot to set up my return. I need you to help me
get back into the village without anyone suspecting I've
returned."

"Oh. Of course. Of course that's what you wanted.
You need to get back into the village." I could sense

some frustration behind her words. Maybe she was getting nervous about being away from the gatehouse so long.

"Will you be here tomorrow?"

"Yes, but not until late. I start work at 5:00 P.M."

"Perfect! The darkness might work to our advantage. I'll probably show up around 9:00 P.M. With a little luck, I'll be in Gram's red sports car. I'll signal you to lift the arm ahead of time so I can race through fast."

"No, Jack. It isn't that simple. You can't just drive back into Paradise!"

"Huh?" Her statement completely startled me. "What do you mean I can't just drive back in? That's how I got in the first time."

"Listen, Jack. When I came to work today, I talked with Mona, one of the ladies who's worked here for several years. She's always telling me how I remind her of her granddaughter, so I decided to get *really* friendly today. Well, when I started asking her questions about the electrical system that surrounds the village, she became very tight-lipped. At first, I thought she wasn't going to answer me. Finally though, she told me a little of what she knew or what she'd heard from other people. I don't really understand it all, but somehow the citizens of Paradise are 'tagged' under the skin somewhere."

My entire body began to itch at the mere suggestion of this "tagging," but I let her continue.

"The *sensor net*, that's what the electrical field is called, can't locate you outside of the village, but when you try to reenter, it will become alerted. You'll receive a shock upon returning if I don't cut the power again. I'm almost certain of it." She took my hand and squeezed it gently.

As usual there were a million questions I wanted to ask. Questions about the sensor net *and* about the tagging, but I had to get moving. Hanging around the gatehouse too long might endanger Jori. "Fine. Then you'll cut the power again – only this time I'll be a little more careful before I go charging through. Better make sure I have my foot firmly on the brake of Gram's hot rod – right?" I grinned at her playfully, but her gaze remained intense.

"Jack, do you think someone will get suspicious? I mean two power outages in two days time? That kind of thing just doesn't happen here."

"Don't worry. It'll be fine. You're doing it so fast that it probably doesn't do anything but make the lights blink for a quick second. No one will even notice." Then I added an afterthought. "I hope." My mind was already back home. I had to find Bill Simpson. He was the one who might be able to help me. Then, I'd . . .

"Well. See you tomorrow?" Jori interrupted my thoughts and stood looking at me expectantly.

"Oh. Sorry. My mind was on the mission. Yeah. Tomorrow. See you then." I turned to go, but she grabbed my arm and spun me around.

"Ohhhh! Jack, honestly."

Yep. I was right. Something was definitely frustrating this girl. I was about to tell her that I really didn't have time for a heart to heart conversation just now when she suddenly placed her hands squarely against my chest and shoved my back up against a tree. Then she pressed in toward me and, before I knew what was happening, my lips were locked in a tremendous form of entertainment. Fireworks seemed to be exploding everywhere. My pulse and heart rate were back to that gymnastics routine they had been rehearsing the first time I ever saw this girl, and I quickly decided that there was indeed time for a heart to heart talk – or anything else she might have in mind. I was about to say as much when she pulled away from me quite suddenly.

"Hey! Wait a minute." I said.

She was heading back to the gatehouse at a brisk pace. She turned and gave me a wry smile. "Serves you right."

"You can't just do that and then . . ." All of a sudden my knees went weak from all of the excitement of the moment. I found myself leaning against the tree for support as I slid toward the ground. "This is humiliating," I said to myself, but I couldn't manage to stand up. "Thank goodness Troy isn't here to see this! I'd never hear the end of it."

A little ingenuity plus the fifty bucks Troy contributed to the cause helped me arrange a bus trip back to Davenport. Troy's majorly wealthy compared to me. He saves money religiously which, if you think about it, is completely inconsistent with nearly every other aspect of his personality. But then that's Troy. He defies any form of rational analysis. He would be a psychiatrist's nightmare. I stepped onto the bus and started laughing as I imagined the trauma Troy would undoubtedly put a counselor through during any type of therapy session. Then, my mind turned to Gram. I wondered about the shock she'd taken. I wondered how serious it was. Would she be up and around by the time I came back tomorrow? That would give her two days of recovery time. I hoped it would be enough. Leaving Paradise wasn't going to be easy if she wasn't up for travel. I shoved my hands deep into my pockets and felt the jingle of keys. Apparently, Gram had decided it would be best to travel with Troy and me during the move to Paradise, so she had left her little red sports car in a garage at AK Printing. Bill Simpson had agreed to look after it until she came to claim it. Well, today was claim day, only I was the claimant – not her. I had taken the keys from her jewelry box without asking, but I knew she would have agreed if she'd been conscious.

Forty-five minutes later I was sitting in the office of Bill Simpson, Chief Executive Officer of AK Printing. While I waited for him to return from lunch, I studied the room. It was warm and inviting. Lots of photographs. What I liked best was that the majority of them were of my grandparents. In fact, there was a 5X7 of Gram sitting right on his desk. I picked up the photo. Her eyes seemed to dance and sparkle with energy just as they would if she were standing in the room.

"A tremendous woman. Gracious, charming, and as lovely today as she was thirty years ago. That's the day I met her." Bill Simpson was standing behind me admiring the photograph I was holding. I hadn't heard him enter the room.

I stood to shake his hand. "Mr. Simpson. Thank you for seeing me on such short notice, Sir."

"Now . . . young man, Jack, isn't it?" He circled to his desk and sat down. "Sit down and stop the pleasantries. When my secretary said Katy Barrett's grandson needed to see me, she'd said enough. Boy, your grandfather was the finest man who ever lived. Amos was my best friend, and Kathryn was his partner in every sense of the word. I may be CEO of this company, Jack, but your grandmother is the Chairman of the Board. I wouldn't have it any other way. She *knows* about people, and *because* she knows about people – *she knows about business*."

I smiled. This was a man I instantly liked. Other than Jori, he was the first comforting soul I'd met since we moved. I could see why my grandparents had always placed so much trust in him.

"Now, what can I do for you, Jack." He eyed me expectantly.

I shifted uncomfortably in my seat. I didn't know where to begin. If I told him everything, he might think I was crazy. I decided to tell him only what was necessary for now. I'd see where that took us. "Gram sent me here, Mr. Simpson. She wanted me to ask you about my father's stock in the company."

Now, *Mr. Simpson* was the one who looked uncomfortable. "Why, Jack, that's something she needs to take up with Chip. I can't be meddling in family affairs. You have Katy call me, and I'll tell her . . ."

I cut him off. "Mr. Simpson there's no time. My grandmother's in trouble. We all are. Except my father maybe. I don't know. Something's happened to him. He's acting bizarre. Gram needs your help. She sent me here so you would help us. Please, Sir." I was trying to keep desperation out of my voice, but even I could hear it seeping through. I was so confused. I didn't even know what I was really asking this man about. What did my father's stock in Gram and Grampa's printing business have to do with anything? He hated the business. Why would he have stock in it? Even if he did, so what? How was that related to what was happening in Paradise? Still, I reminded myself, if Gram needed this information then it *had* to be important.

Mr. Simpson hit a button on his desk. "Lucille, hold all my calls. I'm not to be interrupted until you hear differently."

Now we were getting somewhere. Obviously, Mr. Simpson was going to take action. I watched as he rose from his desk and wandered over to a closet behind me.

"Jack, it's clear that something is not right with this entire situation. Katy would never have sent you to me unless she was in a mess she couldn't get out of on her own, and we all know that's not likely to happen very often to a woman like your grandmother." He chuckled softly. "Now, I'm going to tell you something that up until now only your father and I have ever known." He began shuffling through the closet, but since he was behind me I couldn't see what he was doing. Then, I heard the sound of something ripping. I started to turn in my seat but stopped myself as he began speaking again. I didn't want to appear rude – staring at him – what with him about to take me into his confidence and all.

"Jack, your grandparents gave your father a sizable portion of stock in their company at a fairly young age, and they made certain that he learned about investing and the responsibilities of being a shareholder. Chip, though, wasn't interested in AK Printing. He *was*, however, **interested in making money. When he was thirty-eight,** he came to see me. He wanted to sell me his stock in the company. He wanted out completely. He had plans – dreams of his own. He'd found some land that he was interested in buying over a period of several years. He needed cash – lots of it and fast. Some he would use as a down payment on the land. The rest he would reinvest and try to make fast money in the stock market."

I turned in my chair and looked back toward the closet, but I could only see his back. "Mr. Simpson, did you buy my father's stock?" I heard the ripping sound again. What was he doing? Maybe destroying some important papers to prevent my father from using them in some way?

"Yes, Jack, I bought the stock – and at a fairly hefty price. But I never told your grandparents. It would have crushed them. Oh, they knew their son wasn't interested in the business, but to sell out his own family's stock? I don't believe they would have ever thought he could do such a thing, and I couldn't bring myself to tell them about it. I'm betting that your grandmother has somehow figured out that he sold the stock, though I can't imagine how she became suspicious. It happened such a long time ago." He closed the closet doors, and I turned back in my seat expecting him to return to his desk.

"Maybe *you* know what made her so suspicious all of a sudden, Jack?"

"I'm not sure," I said. "Maybe because he bought this huge, expensive house. I know she wondered where he came up with the money. I never knew anything about this situation with the stock. Now that I know, I'm going to . . ."

"Keep quiet about it. *For a very long time!*" His voice was instantly menacing – nothing at all like the kindly man who had spoken of my grandmother so affectionately only moments before. From behind me his two large hands forced a thick, heavy tape over my mouth – pressing against my lips fast and hard. I was momentarily stunned, but instinct kicked in and I raised my arms to remove it just as he gave me a hard right with his fist. While I reeled from the blow, he pinned my arms behind me and began encircling my wrists with the same heavy tape. I tried to cry out, but it was immediately clear that he had efficiently squelched that plan. The tape over my mouth was so secure that I couldn't utter a grunt much less a cry. I began struggling in the chair, and he dealt me a forceful blow from the left that knocked my chair over completely. I lay motionless for a moment, and somehow thought to close my eyes. I heard him reach across his desk.

"Lucille," he said calmly – as though he'd just finished reading a bedtime story to his grandchild, "get me Chip Barrett on the phone. *And tell him it's urgent.*"

Chapter Fourteen

He clicked the receiver down indicating that he was putting it on speakerphone. Then, I heard him pulling more tape from the roll.

I had only one shot at escaping, and I knew both my timing and my execution would have to be perfect in order for me to succeed. I pulled my knees in toward my chest as far as I could without making it look unnatural. At the same time, I tried to hold my eyes comfortably closed. It was important that Mr. Simpson believe the fall had knocked me unconscious; meanwhile, I was working at the tape around my wrists – pulling it as taut as I could and rubbing it against the corner of the chair. Since my eyes were closed, I could never be sure when he was looking at me, so I moved my arms as slowly as possible.

"Bill, what's the problem?" My father's voice over the speakerphone made me instantly nauseous.

"Chip, I've got a situation here that I am *none* too happy about. One of your boys showed up at my office this afternoon with a whole bunch of questions that made me feel *so* uncomfortable." I heard the sound of more tape ripping and tensed as he approached me. "Now, Chip, I've got the situation entirely under control, of course, but . . ." I felt him reach for my ankles, and as he did I pulled my legs in just a bit more and then let them loose with all the power I could muster. It happened so fast that he had no time to prepare. The soles of my shoes launched directly into his lower abdomen and sent him flying up and over his desk. My momentum carried me into a rather awkward and uncomfortable sitting position, but I was able to see him land hard against the tall bookcase behind his desk. I assumed he'd had the wind knocked out of him, and as he slumped to the ground his head slammed down against the wooden armrest of his chair with a loud "crack."

"Bill? Bill? What's happening?" My father's voice began to panic. "Which of my boys have you got? Bill? Bill! Bill, what's going on over there?"

I jumped up and purposely backed into one of the desk drawers to pull it open. Completely ignoring my father's incessant shouting, I searched through the drawer for scissors which I found and managed to use with a degree of success – only one hand was bleeding before I freed my wrists. Then, I ripped the tape off of my mouth with one broad stroke and slammed my finger onto the speakerphone to disconnect my father. He was almost instantly replaced by the voice of Mr. Simpson's secretary over the intercom.

"Mr. Simpson? I know you said not to disturb you, but I . . . Sir? Is everything all right, Sir? I heard a crash."

I pictured poor Lucille sitting at her desk sweating up a storm and trying to decide whether to enter the office after hearing all of the commotion.

"Mr. Simpson?" Lucille's voice was rising in pitch. I guessed she was about to burst into tears from exasperation. Bill Simpson wasn't stirring; I couldn't even tell if he was *breathing*. Whatever the case, I couldn't risk having Lucille enter the office.

Tap. Tap. She was at the door now. "Please, Mr. Simpson. Oh, *please* answer." She was whining rather pitifully. Poor thing. She was a wreck. I thought about what Troy would likely do in this situation and grinned. I punched the intercom and covered my voice with my hands. Then I coughed intermittently as I spoke.

"Lucille," (cough, cough). "Things are fine, now. I just had a little fall, but I'm fine. Just fine (cough, cough)." I tried to make my voice as deep as possible. Good thing intercoms distort people's voices a little anyway. "Lucille, I'd like you to take the rest of the day off. In fact, take the rest of the week off – with pay!"

"Why Mr. Simpson. That's so generous, Sir. Thank you, but I *couldn't*!"

"Now, Lucille. I'll hear no more about it. I want you out of here in less than five minutes. Go on (cough)! Spend some time with your family! Head over to the mall. Do something nice for yourself."

"Well, Mr. Simpson, if you're *sure*. I mean I feel so funny about this. It isn't National Secretaries' Week or anything."

"Everyday is a day to celebrate a wonderful secretary like you, Lucille. Now I don't want to hear another word about it!" And I didn't. Lucille was too loyal for her own good.

Finally, I heard the sound of a file cabinet opening and closing, then a closet. Moments later she was gone, and I breathed a sigh of relief while yanking the phone cord out of the wall. Next, I grabbed his pen and reached for his notepad, but then I had a better idea. I threw the notepad in the garbage can and scrawled right on his fancy leather desk pad in big bold letters. "I gave Lucille the rest of the week off – *with pay*. She's overworked."

Then, I left his office, rendered Lucille's phone inoperative and, with some major muscle work, moved her desk and other office furniture up against his door. When Mr. Simpson did finally regain consciousness, he'd be busy trying to get out of that office for a while.

Finding Gram's car was no problem. She and Grampa Amos each had a space in the heated garage attached to the south end of the plant. I noted Grampa's space was now designated by a sign as Mr. Simpson's. I started the engine of Gram's car, hit the door opener, and flew out into traffic at a respectable speed. There was no time to let the car warm up. I had a lot to do and very little time to work with. I could only imagine what my father was doing or thinking right now, and that meant time was not on my side.

As I pulled out of the parking lot and headed toward the highway, I couldn't stop thinking about Bill Simpson. How could my grandparents have been so wrong about someone?   Was he involved with my father and Mr. Eden? Or was he simply trying to protect the secret that he had bought my father's stock? And if so, why? No answers came. I drove down Park Boulevard, one of the main drags through our town, and was comforted by familiar sights.   Some people would say there was no comparison between Davenport and Paradise, and they'd be right. One was reality. The other was *fantasy* – the dark kind.

I was a quarter mile past the sign before my mind registered what it had said. I made a sharp right with no time for a signal – the tires squealed superbly – Gram knew how to pick out transportation! Two more rights and a left put me back on the boulevard headed in the opposite direction. *Wakefield Monument Company.* I had never noticed it before. I felt the receipt in my pocket. It was my only connection to Mr. Eden. I had no idea what a monument company was or why Mr. Eden might have done business there, but I was more than a little interested to find out. Was he having some kind of statue made for his village? If so, this stop might turn out to be an enormous waste of what I didn't have much of – time. I parked, if you could call it that, and raced into the building. I was no more than two steps in the door when the sight of the first headstone paralyzed me. As I stood there taking it all in, a sense of foreboding came over me like nothing I had ever known. Suddenly, I knew what a monument company was. This room was completely filled with headstones for *burial* plots.

A girl who looked to be in her early twenties stepped forward and introduced herself. "Hi, I'm Denise. You look a little younger than our typical clients, but I'd be happy to help you if I can."

I fumbled for the receipt and finally managed to hand it to her. Then, I tried out a story I'd had very little time to work up. "Yes . . . well, my father sent me over. You see, we received a bill this past week, but he had this receipt showing that he'd already paid you. My father's a very busy man. He asked me to stop by and clear up the matter."

She smiled. I must have been convincing. Lies often sound better coming out than they do when you're working them out in your head. "Well, this should be easy enough to clear up," she said walking through two small doors that were waist-high and which were clearly placed there to keep customers out of the office area. I watched as she went to her desk and pulled a large black binder to the edge. She flipped through several pages looking for a document to match the receipt and seemed at last to find one. Then, she grabbed a blue binder and began searching through that one. Waiting takes longer when you don't really know what the person you're waiting for is doing. At last, she rose from her desk and approached the counter area where I moved to meet her.

"All solved," she said. "Your father must not have checked the bill carefully. We billed him for the *new* order he placed last week. This receipt you've brought in is for an old order."

"But this receipt is less than a week old." I looked at the date on the receipt again. I was really confused. "You consider that *old?*"

"No, no. I don't mean that the receipt is old. I mean the *order* is old. It's not uncommon these days for people to buy burial plots or to order headstones ahead of time. That receipt is for a headstone that was ordered nearly a month ago. The stone was just delivered to the cemetery this past week. My records show that someone stopped in and paid for it on the same day it was delivered to the cemetery, and the receipt was issued then. Did you have a chance to see the headstone?"

I was trying to slow my thoughts down enough to seize the moment and gather some information. So, Mr. Eden was headstone shopping. Who for? "Uhhh, yeah! I saw it. It was fine. And you, uhhh . . . even spelled the first name right, too. That's not always the case, of course." I was fishing – would she bite? Yes! She looked back at her book then turned to me quizzically. She didn't bite exactly. She swallowed me whole.

"Well, I appreciate the compliment, but how many different ways are there to spell *Susan?*"

The air around me became increasingly warm, and I leaned forward on the counter.

"Sir? You look dizzy. Are you okay? Would you like to sit down?"

"Wh . . . wh . . . was her name Susan *Barrett*?" The words came haltingly from my mouth as if they were daggers that were leaving my throat and gums bloodied and raw.

My discomfort was now painfully apparent, and she was instantly uncomfortable. "Well, *yes*. Yes, it was. Didn't you know? I'm so sorry. I assumed . . . I mean, since your father . . . Well, when you made that comment about the spelling, I thought that . . ."

It's amazing how much a human being can endure when called upon to do so. Looking back, I'm not sure what kept me from collapsing in sobs in front of that poor girl right then and there. I had no way of being sure that my mother was truly dead, so I decided to cling to the hope that she was alive somewhere, somehow. I turned – thinking that I would race to the cemetery to see for myself, when a portion of our earlier conversation finally sunk in. My eyes locked on hers.

"You said he placed a *new* order last week Who, exactly placed the order?" I didn't give her a chance to answer before launching the next question with even more intensity. "What does the headstone read?" My fear and potential grief over Mom was tabled for the moment because I had a strong feeling that Mr. Eden had them carving away on a memorial stone for my brother.

She glanced toward the blue binder that was still lying open on her desk. "I'm not sure I should be discussing all of this information with you. Perhaps you could wait here a moment while I speak with our manager." She was definitely becoming suspicious.

I vaulted over the swinging doors and moved to grab the binder, but she met me at the desk and forcibly placed both hands on the binder. "Sir, I can't allow you to go through private records without proper identification, and even then . . ."

"No problem," I gripped both of her wrists tightly and backed her up to a chair. "I'm not asking!" A quick shove seated her for just long enough. I ripped the page from the binder and ran. By the time she reached the parking lot, I was moving into traffic at a speed that would have done Gram proud. I needed somewhere to think, somewhere to be quiet for just a few minutes. There was too much coming at me too fast. My great "plan" was a shambles. Before I realized it, I was on Wabash Avenue, and my old house was less than a block away. The mind is an incredible instrument. Mine sought out a safe place. I pulled over, intending to park and look over the document I'd taken from Wakefield, when I was startled by a *For Sale* sign in our yard. Did the new owners decide to sell already?

Something was nagging at me. Who *were* the new owners? Gram had asked. She was interested in whether they had children, and Dad had shut her down fast. I remembered the conversation clearly thanks to my "ear to the floor and door" maneuver when they were in the study. Then, all at once, I knew. There were no new owners. The house had never been sold. And Gram had figured it out, too. That's why she wanted to know about his stock. She had been suspicious before about how my father could afford the house in Paradise when she saw it – even with Mr. Eden's supposed generous pricing. But if this house hadn't even been sold, my father surely couldn't have afforded a new one.

Instinct told me I should park around the corner and walk back to the house. I don't always follow my instincts, but this time I did. It turned out to be a *very* good idea because, as it turned out, I wasn't the only visitor to the house that afternoon. I grabbed the paper from Wakefield, purposely left the car unlocked and the key in the ignition (instinct again), made a speedy trip to the front porch, and found that the house was vacant. I raced to the back and found my secret key buried not too far under a stepping-stone in Gram's rose garden. In the haste of the move, I had left it. As I jammed the key into the lock, I could feel my repressed emotions making their way to the surface. I needed just a few minutes of solitude to get myself together. The moments of comfort I was seeking proved evasive, however, as soon as I looked at the paper I'd carried inside.

The form from Wakefield Monument Company that I'd assumed was one piece of paper was actually two stapled pages. I hadn't realized it until now. It was made of a thin "tissuey" kind of paper. The kind that rips if you don't write on it very gently. I skimmed the first page in search of Troy's name, certain that I would find it.

Certain that . . . "*Kathryn Barrett*." I said the words aloud, and they echoed through the empty rooms of the house and flew back at me with surprising force. I sat down on the smooth hardwood floor and leaned against the side of a kitchen cabinet. I had been expecting Troy's name – had never considered that anyone *else* was Mr. Eden's target. Anyone else? I ripped page one away. The second page was actually a faxed order. The date and time indicated that it had been sent that very day – only a few minutes before I had arrived at Wakefield.

My eyes already knew which line held the information I sought. I glanced down quickly as if speed would lessen the effect of what was recorded there. And then, in what has become a moment I've relived time and again, I saw a second headstone ordered. "*Jack Edward Barrett*." My father's signature stood out prominently at the bottom of the form.

Chapter Fifteen

"Well," I spoke out loud even though I was my only audience. "It seems Daddy's figured out which of his boys made it out of Paradise. The prize, however, leaves a lot to be desired." I was moving to stand when I heard a sound that made me more than a little anxious. A car turned into the driveway. Knowing that people who enter driveways frequently enter houses as well, I dropped to all fours and moved like lightning across the floor to the nearest hiding place – the basement. *The basement.* Wouldn't you know it. For someone who hates being underground, I'd been on an awful lot of basement excursions lately. I made a mental note to build my own home on a concrete slab foundation with no basement whatsoever. That way if I should ever again happen to be hiding from psychopathic nutcases who were trying to murder my entire family, I would at least have the satisfaction of knowing that they could not force me into the basement. Well, that was indeed a pleasant thought. I felt much better – until I heard the door to the house open and footsteps approach the basement door.

Of course, I was only standing on the stairs to the basement. No reason to go *all the way down* if it wasn't really necessary, my school of thought suggested. I now came to two startling realizations – one, that basements are a dandy alternative to being discovered by maniacal killers and two, that my school of thought is sometimes a bit flawed. I looked down the stairs. There wasn't nearly enough time to get down. The footsteps stopped by the basement door. I held my breath as the knob turned. The door flew open.

"AAAAAHHHHHHHHH!" I yelled instinctively. Simultaneously, I was greeted with another, even louder, and very high-pitched scream.

"AAAAAAAAHHHHHHHHH!"

I stared at her. "Who are you?" The woman who stood before me gave a whole new definition to the word "unique." She was clad in a leather miniskirt and matching vest that were bright pink in color with yellow stripes running horizontally across them. Her turtleneck sweater was a strong shade of red that clashed terribly with the pink vest. She wore large gold hoop earrings, and she had plastic combs (lime green) pulling back long platinum hair that was full of gel. White tube socks pulled to just below her knees and black leather sandals rounded out her attire.

She chomped on a huge wad of gum that was, unfortunately, all too visible when she talked. "Whatdaya mean who am I? I'm the realtor. Mimi Rosenfeld. Pleased to meetcha!"

I wasn't too thrilled with Mimi at first – even less so when I shook her hand. It had all the firmness of pudding. "I'm Jack Barrett. I live here. I mean, I *used* to."

"Oh, I know how that goes, kid. I'm the same way. *Sentimental fool* they call me. A house is a terribly hard thing to let go of. Ya just had ta take another looksee, huh?"

I had a feeling they called Mimi a lot of things besides sentimental fool, but that wasn't important at the moment. "Yeah. I couldn't help myself. Just had to see the place one more time. Well, I'll be going now. Sorry if I startled you." I stepped off the basement stairs and moved past her.

"Hey, no problem, kid. I just have ta come by once a week and check the house over. I always start at the bottom and work my way up. Ya know, it ain't none of my business, well, actually it *is* my business 'cause real estate is what I do. Just got my license last month. But you oughta tell your pop that leavin' all that stuff locked up in the master bedroom ain't such a good idea. Buyers want to see the master bedroom and imagine how it will look with *their* stuff in it."

I spun on my heels. "Huh? What do you mean?"

Mimi looked exasperated. "*Upstairs.* All them computers and stuff. He keeps 'em locked up in that room, and he won't let me show no one the room. I've left him several messages about it – 'cause it could be a real problem if I had an interested buyer, but he don't get back to me."

"How do you know what's in there?" I questioned.

She dangled her keychain in my face. "Oh, he gave *me* a key, but I ain't supposed to let anyone else in there. I just open the room up and make sure none of his equipment's been tampered with during the night. That's what he told me to do. It's always fine. I don't go inside very far though." She elbowed me. "I ain't much one for *technology,* if ya know what I mean. Anyways, if he wants to sell the house, he needs to listen to me and let people in that room. Maybe you could talk to him – huh, kid?"

Some fast talking convinced Mimi that I would not only persuade my father to listen to her advice, but that I'd check the house over for her and drop the keys back off at her office. I think I had her out of the house in less than five minutes. Clearly my father had selected her because there was no way she'd interfere with whatever he was doing here. There was also very little chance she'd ever sell the house.

I mounted the stairs two at a time, unlocked the doors to the master bedroom, and threw them open with force. Mimi was right. There were five computer monitors on a round table just inside the door and a large central processing unit in the center of the room. There were several phone lines, a fax machine, scanners, and printers scattered throughout the room. I moved the mouse near one of the monitors, and one of the downtown streets of Paradise appeared. The screen flashed "74 degrees" in the upper right hand corner. "What's the story here?" I said to the empty room.

Click. It came from downstairs. Someone had entered the house. Mimi again? I hurriedly reset the lock and dashed out of the room and into the bathroom across the hall. Then, I heard a deep cough. A man had entered the house. Heavy footsteps treaded the stairs, and in a moment the black coat and hat of Mr. Eden passed by my hiding place. I watched as he hurriedly unlocked the door and entered my parents' old bedroom. He closed the door firmly, but I wasn't going to let that stop me. Darting into the hall, I listened near the door. I could hear a chair wheeling around the room, and his fingers were pounding furiously at a keyboard. Then he began to speak in that same deep ominous tone I'd heard when he took Troy from his room. I dropped to the floor and pressed my ear to the open space at the bottom of the door.

"*Jack* has become a problem. You said he wouldn't be any trouble. You *assured* me that you could control him."

"I *can* control him, Adam, usually." My father's voice. My father? But when did he enter the house? How did he get inside the room? "Jack's never been a problem before. Troy – *he's* the problem. Undisciplined, arrogant, rebellious. I've tried to tell you . . ."

"SHUT UP! You ignorant fool. Troy is superior. *Superior*! Hand-eye coordination, muscle tone, reflexes, intelligence, appearance – all perfect. His temperament is being refined little by little each night. Soon, he'll be the perfect son. *My* perfect son."

As Mr. Eden's voice grew in strength, my father's became pleading – almost childlike. "But Adam, Jack's a good boy. He's so much like . . ."

"You." He hissed at my father. "He's like you – weak! Fool-ish-and-weak. Mr. Eden emphatically fired the words forward in single syllables like four deadly bullets that he knew would hit their mark. "Jack has to be dealt with quickly. You've made the arrangements at the cemetery?"

"Yes, Adam, I've made them. But isn't there some other way? Not Jack. I never meant for Jack to be hurt. We agreed. Remember? We agreed that Jack could stay. Only Jack."

"That was before the old woman started poking and prying. She has him placing us in a very dangerous situation. Have you found her yet?"

"That situation is being taken care of – I can *assure* you, Adam. And we'll find Jack. He'll come back to Paradise. He wouldn't leave Troy and my mother."

"Well, when he does, we'll be ready for him. Keep a close eye on the girl. He's bound to reenter the village on her watch. Make certain he gets inside, and let him proceed to the house. Then, see that *she's* taken care of."

"Yes, Adam."

"I have to get back to the village. I want Troy *secured* before anything goes wrong."

"Yes, Adam."

I scurried back to my hiding place across the hall on all fours. A few moments passed with what appeared to be a complete lack of conversation. Then, the door opened and surprisingly, *my father* appeared. I had been expecting Mr. Eden to exit since he had indicated a need to return to Paradise and *secure* Troy – which didn't sound good for Troy. My father made his way down the hall. I heard him descend the stairs and exit the house. A moment later I heard a car start up and back out of our driveway. The window in this bathroom gave me a terrific view of our neighbor, Mrs. Norman's, vegetable garden, but unfortunately it kept me from seeing which way my father went. Hopefully, nowhere near Gram's car.

I waited for the doorknob to turn again. It did not. Then, another thought struck me. If Mr. Eden had been the one to park in the driveway and enter the house, then how did *my father's* car get in the driveway? I reviewed the facts again, trying to make sense of it all. There were no cars in the driveway when I arrived, and only one, discounting Mimi's, had come since I had been here – Mr. Eden's. Yet, my father had just left, and I had clearly heard a car pulling *out* of the driveway just now. Did my father *take* Mr. Eden's car without asking? Furthermore, *where* had my father been the whole time I was in this house? How did he get *into* this house without my knowing about it? For that matter, how did he get *to* this house? Plus, *where* was Mr. Eden, and how was he going to return to Paradise if he let my father take his car? I couldn't seem to create plausible answers for any of my questions.

I stepped cautiously into the hall and moved to listen at the door again. Nothing. I waited five minutes. Nothing. I had to risk it. I turned the doorknob gingerly and jumped when it snapped loudly as it unfastened. I entered the room much as I had before. Things looked the same. There was no sign of Mr. Eden. I searched the master bathroom quietly. *Empty.* There was only one other place he could be. I eyed my parents' huge walk-in closet. The door was closed. My thoughts were wild and outlandish. Could the closet contain a secret passageway from this house to Paradise? Ridiculous. Paradise was forty miles from here. Could Mr. Eden have "transported" to Paradise like characters in sci-fi movies do? No, as much as I hated to admit it, this was reality. I looked out the second story windows as I neared the closet. There was no way he could have left that way. The roof was too slanted. Besides, why would a man who'd recently walked into the house and up to this room like he owned the place, leave it by any other means?

I was tired of endless questions that seemed to have no answers. I was tired of being scared. I grabbed the door handle and yanked it open expecting – I don't know what. I certainly wasn't expecting what I found. I flipped on the light. The closet was nearly empty. All of the shelving had been removed and the drywall replaced so that everything looked as good as new. The walls had even been repainted. At the very back of the closet were two hooks – the smaller positioned slightly above the larger. On the first hook hung Mr. Eden's black trench coat. Just above it, on the second hook, hung his hat.

Chapter Sixteen

I searched every inch of the closet and then the entire room for a secret exit of some kind. It was no use. Mr. Eden had left the room *without* his hat and coat, but I had no idea how he'd managed it. It was getting late. I was tired, hungry, and also nervous about staying in the house for the night. What if Mr. Eden came back? And what about Troy? What was Mr. Eden planning to do with him? What had he meant when he'd said Troy would be *his* son? My feet led me to Gram's old set of rooms while I pondered the strange conversation I'd overheard between my father and Mr. Eden. My father, who had seemed so powerful since going to work for Eden, had sounded so frail during their dialogue. And I couldn't get out of my mind the way he had seemed to be trying to *protect* me. At one point he was almost begging Mr. Eden to let me *stay*. What did that mean? Stay what? *Alive*? That would seem the most likely answer to fill in the blank, but it didn't do much to bolster my spirits. When the same man who's pleading for your life is also ordering a headstone for your burial plot, you need to look elsewhere for a support system.

I walked across the marble floors of Gram's "living room." She had insisted on marble – imported from someplace in Asia. My father had called it a "worthless extravagance" right to her face. She'd simply cocked an eyebrow and retorted, "Yes. I suppose it is, Chip. Fortunately, you don't have to order it, install it, or pay for it. Don't worry so much, Dear. It shortens the life span." She'd then suggested he take a ride with her on her motorcycle. He'd simply frowned and walked away.

I made my way to the set of triple windows which overlooked Gram's rose garden. She'd had exterior lights installed to illuminate her rose bushes at night, and although I was sure a close inspection would reveal their recent lack of care, they looked terrific from this distance. As I paced the empty rooms of my grandmother's old apartment, family videos began to play in my head. Many of them contained my mother; I heard the salesgirl say her name again. *"Susan."* The tears I'd been holding back all day came rushing forth. Soon, my body trembled as I sobbed aloud and hugged my knees to my chest. I'm not ashamed to say it. That was the moment when I admitted to myself that I would probably never see my mother again. I truly believed they had killed her, and tomorrow I would know for sure.

Exhaustion must have swept over me during my breakdown because I awoke in a very uncomfortable position on Gram's marble floor. Sunlight was filtering into the room, and the sense of hope that a new day often brings infected me. My watch read 1:00 P.M. which at first seemed impossible; however, when I thought about

all I'd been through – including several restless nights – I
reasoned that I probably needed the rest. I glanced a few
feet away and saw the withered remains of the rose my
father had destroyed in this room on the day of the move.
I picked it up and wondered where Gram was right now.
Mr. Eden had asked my father if he had *found* her. That
meant she had felt a need to "disappear." But why? And
to where? Did Troy know where she was? Had he
helped to hide her? She was far too weak, in my opinion,
to have done much in the way of travel on her own. I
looked out the windows at the rose garden again and
smiled. I could do something for Gram even if I wasn't
with her. I trotted out of the room and down the steps
feeling more refreshed than I had in days. Hope does that
to you. I picked a rose in full bloom and returned to
Gram's apartment where I promptly opened one window.

My father had interrupted Gram's tradition; I would
finish it for her. Even though I didn't know the story
behind it, I'd seen her perform it a thousand times. All
she had ever said about it was, "It's meant for special
occasions." Well, today *was* a special occasion. I was
returning to Paradise, and I'd be leaving again – with my
brother and my grandmother. We wouldn't *ever* be going
back. I held the rose out into the autumn air and blew
softly until a petal released. Then, I watched as the wind
carried it away. Gram always pressed her roses for a few
days before they went into her scrapbook; I didn't have
that kind of time, but under the circumstances I figured
half a tradition was better than none.

Cemeteries are quiet. They're also lonely. Davenport only had one cemetery, and I'd visited it many times since Grampa's death. I knew my way around the place because Gram came each month with a rose, and she always brought either Troy or me. Sometimes we both came.

I saw the fresh mound of dirt while I was still a good distance away from it, but it didn't lessen the pain of standing over it. *Susan Reilly Barrett*, it read. *Beloved Wife and Mother*. Beloved wife. I looked scornfully at the two large potted plants on either side of the headstone and bent down to read the cards. One read "Always a part of me, never apart from me, Chip." The other was simply Mr. Eden's business card. Rage welled up within me that went completely unchecked. "YOU MONSTERS! MURDERERS! YOU *KILLED* MY MOTHER!" I smashed the first pot against the base of the gravestone with tremendous force, and jagged shards went flying in all directions. The second one was obliterated in a similar manner – chipping away a piece of the headstone as well. "I'LL GET YOU! Both of you! You *can't* destroy my family. I won't let you!" I dropped to one knee, breathing heavily, and surveyed the damage. Bits of plant, soil, and ceramic were scattered in all directions. That new sense of hope I'd experienced earlier had evaporated.

The hot tears running down my face began to form small pools in the dirt below. I knelt on the grass next to her grave. "Ohhh, Mom. Mom, *I'm sorry*. I didn't

know. None of us did. We could have protected you . . .
warned you . . . but we didn't know. We couldn't have
known. He's *crazy*, Mom. They're *both* crazy. They're
out of their minds. And Dad *hates* Troy, but I don't know
why. And now, Mom, now he's going to get rid of Gram
and *me, too*. Just like you. Dad's planning to have us
murdered."

You can only stay in a cemetery for so long. After
about an hour, I left and spent the remainder of the day
visiting with our old next-door neighbor, Mrs. Norman,
and playing with her dog, Benny. She called me "sweet
and sentimental" when I told her I just had to visit the old
neighborhood one more time and then gave me lemonade
and some of her homemade sugar cookies. I mowed her
lawn, and she invited me to stay for dinner. By the time
she'd finished telling me about all five of her
grandchildren and showing me the slides of her Japanese
missionary friends, it was a little after 8:00 P.M. – time to
head back to Paradise.

The earlier conversation between my father and Mr.
Eden indicated that they were going to allow Jori to help
me reenter the village. Mr. Eden knew I would head for
the house, and I had the feeling he wanted me to go there.
It was clear, however, from his conversation with my
father, that once I left the gatehouse area, Jori would be in
danger. Luckily, *they* didn't know that *I* knew their plan.
Best of all, I had developed a plan of my own. Jori
wasn't staying in that gatehouse. When the power went

off in Paradise, my "gatehouse girlfriend" as Troy called her, was coming with me. Let somebody else worry about turning the power back on. She'd be safely inside the village before that happened.

The trip to Paradise was uneventful. To tell the truth, I was so caught up in thinking about seeing Jori again that the time flew. Of course, driving Gram's car also helped time to fly. I was doing close to 100 M.P.H. on two occasions. It's easy to speed when you've been riding with my grandmother for most of your life. Reminding myself that a speeding ticket would throw my timetable way off motivated me to bring the speedometer down to a more reasonable figure. Gram says 85 is as reasonable a figure as any she's ever heard of, but I decided to stick with something I felt the police would view as reasonable.

The decrepit sign welcoming people to Paradise and the small brick gatehouse were exactly as I'd left them. As I pulled up to the window where I first met her, Jori leaned out and grinned. "*You* certainly didn't waste any time getting back here."

I smiled. "When there's someone so pleasant to come back to, I usually rush." There was a brief pause, and then we both spoke the same words at the same time!

"That sounds just like something Troy would say!"

We started giggling and I grabbed Jori's hand tightly and lowered my voice. "Jori, listen carefully. You're in danger. Serious danger. Is my grandmother's makeup bag still inside the gatehouse?"

"Makeup bag?" She looked at me curiously. "Jack, there's only . . ."

We didn't have time for this. "The case. The little luggage tote – she calls it her . . . never mind. Get it. Open it. Is there anything in there that you can use to keep the power off?"

The urgency of my voice seemed to motivate her. She grabbed Gram's makeup bag, and I could hear her rapidly going through the contents. "Wow! She's got a signed picture of *Elvis* in here. Is this authentic, Jack?"

"Jori!"

"Sorry! I know, I know – *hurry*. Okay, what about Super Glue? She's got some of that. Why don't I put it all over the pad where the lever rests when I pull it down?"

"That's great! Do it. Then get in the car with me."

She lifted the mechanical arm that would allow Gram's car to enter the village and left it in the raised position. I waited for her to pull the lever. I still hadn't figured out what they had done to me while I was in Paradise that made it impossible for me to come and go from the village at will. I entered this village several days ago with no problem, yet Jori had assured me that I could not do so again without receiving megavolts – possibly enough to kill me. The lever went down, and all lights inside Paradise went dark. The entire city. Jori rounded the corner and jumped into the car. I kicked the engine, and we sped off to the house not knowing for sure what awaited us.

On the short drive to the house, I briefed Jori on the details of my crazy life. The fact that she didn't jump out of the car and scream for help was a good sign. I told her all about "Mom" and Bill Simpson. I also told her what had happened to my real mother – making it clear that now was not the time to discuss the subject in any detail. I needed to be on top of my game for what was coming next. She smiled warmly when I told her about what I'd done with Gram's rose, and then she grinned and patted something on the seat next to her. Keeping my hands firmly on the wheel, I looked over to see what it was. "Gram's makeup bag! You brought it!"

"A woman should never be without her makeup bag, Jack. Besides, I want to ask her about that picture of Elvis."

When I reached the house, I pulled the car around and backed into our driveway just far enough to get us off the street. I'm not sure why, but I didn't want the car too close to the house. Instinct again. I shut off the engine and lights. We were now encased in total darkness except for the light that the moon provided. "Well, here we are. Just so you know, tonight probably won't be what I would typically plan for a first date."

She reached across the seat and kissed me lightly on the cheek. "I'll forgive you, Jack. As long as you promise there'll be other dates."

There went those fireworks again. I opened the car door and rushed around to get hers just as she opened it – right into my left leg. I was on the ground again.

"Owwww! Ahhhh! Gee!" The fingers of both hands laced involuntarily around my left shin. It felt like the corner of her car door had sliced directly into it.

"Oh, Jack, I'm so sorry. And you were trying to be such a gentleman and open the door for me. It's so dark. I didn't realize you were coming, and I . . . oh, does it hurt much?" She pulled Gram's makeup bag out of the car. "Should I look for something to put on it?"

"No." I gritted my teeth. "No, no. It's fine. I just got knocked off balance for a minute." That's all I needed. Jori was going to doctor up my boo-boo! She helped me up, and I leaned against the car for a minute.

"You know," she started, "this whole thing – I mean the two of us . . . together. I can hardly believe it. All the girls at my school are so jealous whenever I talk about what a hunk Mr. Eden's older son is."

Hunk. Did she say *hunk*? She called me a *hunk*. This was a good thing. Yes. I liked the sound of that. *I* was the hunk. Not Troy. Me. There had been no mention of Troy whatsoever in the *hunk* category, and I had been listening very carefully. All at once it hit me – first like a cottonball and then like a brick. "Jori, I'm not *Mr. Eden's* son. Whatever gave you that idea?"

The moonlight caught her face so that I could see her mouth form a wry grin. "Okay fine, Jack. You're *not* Mr. Eden's son. Then *why* was he the one driving you into Paradise the day we first met, and *why* did you refer to the man driving that car as your father? You even apologized for his behavior!"

"Jori!" I placed my hands on her shoulders. "Somehow you've got this all confused. My father is *Chip Barrett*. I'm Jack Barrett. My father *works* for Mr. Eden, but Mr. Eden *isn't* my father. I've never personally met the man! I've never even seen his face!"

Abruptly, she pulled away from me, and her tone became very firm. "Look, Jack. I don't know what's going on here. This whole story you've been telling me about your family – is *any* of it real? Because if it isn't, then you'd better tell me right now. I've been working at that gatehouse for two years. I've seen Mr. Eden enter and leave Paradise hundreds of times. I think I know what he looks like by now! You can call your father anything you want to, but I'll tell you one thing – the man who drove you into Paradise *was* Mr. Eden."

Chapter Seventeen

"Jori, I've been truthful with you about everything, and I'm being truthful with you now. Mr. Eden is *not* my father."

She began drumming her fingers on the edge of the car. "Then how do you explain . . ."

I grabbed her hand and headed for the house. "I can't explain it, and we can't stay in one place this long." As we made our way silently up the long driveway and eventually into the yard, I was trying to come up with a reasonable explanation for Jori's assertion that I was Mr. Eden's son. She kept referring to the day we came to Paradise. I tried to relive that day in my mind. The thing I remembered most vividly was seeing *her* for the first time. I remembered Troy had made a play for her, and Gram had silenced him. And Dad. Dad had been rude to her, and that had embarrassed me. What had he done? She had been in the process of greeting him, *and he had cut her off.* Yes. She had said, "Good afternoon, Mr. . . ." and he had interrupted her. At the time I thought he was being rude because he was in a hurry. Thinking about it now – if Jori had been allowed to finish her greeting, she would have said, "Good afternoon, Mr. *Eden!*" Why? Because she knew him as Mr. Eden. My father knew that was what she was about to say, and that's why he had interrupted her. Likewise, she must have been about to reveal something else he didn't want us to hear because he suddenly shot the car forward and nearly crippled the mechanical arm. He had then insisted on taking the paperwork back to her, despite my clear desire to do so. *He didn't want me talking to her.*

As Jori and I crossed the large expanse of lawn in front of the house, I thought about the night I'd found Troy missing from his room. After searching the house, I'd seen the door to my parents' bedroom closing. Then, I'd found Troy back in bed. I assumed that Dad, the impostor, or both had taken him and returned him. However, the next time I was aware of it happening, it had been Mr. Eden who had removed him, but I *had not followed Mr. Eden out of the room or seen him exit the house.* I'd been too worried about Troy. What if he never left? What if he returned to my parents' bedroom because . . . I began breaking out in a cold sweat as flashbacks of every memory regarding my father and Mr. Eden began cascading through my mind. The house in Davenport. The closet. The hooks. That coat and hat.

"Jori." I came to a dead stop. "In Davenport yesterday – Mr. Eden . . . he came to the house. He went into a room, but *my father* left the room. I looked for Mr. Eden in the room . . . there was no way he could have gotten out of that room. His hat. And his coat. I found his hat and coat, but *he* wasn't there! He'd already left! He'd walked right past me!"

The tone of my voice and the way my words were spilling out made my revelation an incoherent mess to her. "Jack. Slow down. I don't understand. Are you saying that . . ."

"I'm saying that you're right. *My father is Mr. Eden. They're the same person!*" As an afterthought, I added, "He must have forgotten to mention it."

My attempt at humor was wasted because every fiber of my being was screaming that this could not be possible. The phone calls to our house, the beeper going off. It was *Mr. Eden* calling, right? That's what we'd been *told*. But how difficult would it be to arrange such things? And the stock. Mr. Simpson had said that Dad had sold the stock because he needed a lot of money to buy some land. *Paradise.* He was buying the land for this village. All these years, ever since he was twenty-one, my father had been reinvesting stocks, making big money, and buying more and more land. He'd built this village. He'd built The Garden School. All of this was some kind of sick, twisted world he'd created.

I thought back to my father's phone conversation with Mr. Eden before we moved – the one I had purposely stayed in the dining room to witness. Was there no one at the other end of the phone line? Had he been having a "pretend" conversation? Worse yet – did he *think* there was someone on the other end of the line talking to him when there really *wasn't* anyone there at all? Now that was a scary thought. Oh yeah. Let's not even dwell on that idea because *that* would mean that my father wasn't just your regular run-of-the-mill, power-obsessed, workaholic, plot-the-murder-of-three-family-members-in-less-than-a-month, loony toon. No, that would mean that my father was *insane.* Yet, insanity was the only explanation, and it was locked at the forefront of my thoughts. Why? Because of what I had overheard yesterday. Mr. Eden and my father were involved in a heated argument, and I had heard every word of it. There was no denying it. Two distinctly different voices coming from within one man. *He had been arguing with himself!* Two personalities. One man. It was the only possible explanation, and it fit like a glove. I grabbed Jori's hand again and bolted toward the side of the house. I had viewed each man as a major force to be reckoned with – now that I had made this discovery, I was certain that they? . . . he? . . . *It?* . . . was capable of anything.

We stepped onto the screened porch that led directly to the kitchen. I decided, at this point, to spare Jori the details of just exactly how crazy my father actually was. Maybe we could still come out of this mess with her in a less-than-panicked state regarding the Barrett gene pool. All at once, the house lit up. Apparently power had been restored. Was it *chance* that it should happen just as we arrived at the house? I released Jori's hand. "Stay close by me . . . and follow my lead whatever I do. Even if it doesn't make sense. Okay?" At least I *sounded* heroic. My knees were knocking, but I didn't think she could hear them.

"Whatever you say, Sir." She saluted. "Hey, did I tell you I'm a green belt in karate? You just give the word, and I'll take somebody down. You know I threw my instructor right into the . . . "

I was peering into the kitchen and trying desperately to pretend that my girlfriend was not revealing that her alter ego was *Wonder Woman*. I turned from the window and put my finger to my lips. "Ssshh! Something's happening." Actually, nothing was happening, but I didn't want to hear that she'd probably hospitalized her karate instructor. A guy's ego can only take so much. *Give the word.* Jeez! What did she think, that I was going to have her beat up the bad guys and save me? I let that thought pass quickly by. The thought of life with Troy, should Jori manage to be *my* hero, was beyond what any human could ever be expected to endure.

Another look into the kitchen revealed dear old "Mom," dressed as usual for the Mrs. America pageant, getting out the cutting board. We watched as she went about meticulously seasoning some meat. I decided it was time for action. Of course, what kind of action was anyone's guess, so I went with something totally new and innovative. I was taking the entire "hero returns to the villain's hideout" scenario in a whole new direction with this move – I tapped on the window and smiled.

She scurried to the door in her high-heeled shoes and opened it invitingly. "Jack, darling. *Wherever* have you been? I've been so worried. You're supposed to tell your family if you're leaving the house. *Everyone knows that.*"

She ruffled my hair. "Well, I'm just glad you're home." She turned to look at Jori. "And *who* is this precious thing?"

"I'm . . ."

I jumped in. "She's *Mary,* Mom. You know from *Mary had a little lamb.*"

Jori looked at me curiously, and I winked.

"Mom" just stared at us. There was a long, awkward pause. Then, she moved back to the cutting board and began chopping away at some tenderloin with a meat cleaver. She did not respond.

I motioned for Jori to stay back while I moved in for the kill. "Mom, you know *Mary* don't you? She's *Mary* from the nursery rhyme. Have you seen her lamb, Mom?"

Her head remained down, and her eyes were focused solely on the meat. She was hacking away. Chopping, slicing, dicing. One wrong move and she'd be down to four fingers. That cleaver was sharp.

I started chanting. *"Mary had a little lamb, its fleece was white as snow, And everywhere that Mary went the lamb was sure to go."* Then I switched gears on her. *"Mary, Mary, quite contrary, how does your garden grow? With . . ."*

Her body began to tremble – kind of an involuntary shudder. She raised the cleaver over the meat again but held it poised in midair as another shudder surged through her body. I was getting to her. My plan was working. "What's wrong, *Mom*? What are you doing?"

Instantaneously, she whirled on me with teeth bared and a savage snarl on her lips. "Just slicing some *meat!*" The cleaver was in motion with tremendous force before I could anticipate it. I jumped back but felt the cold steel connect with my skin.

"Jack!" Jori's face was contorted in a look of disbelief and horror. I looked down. The cleaver had sliced midway across my chest. A fairly large section of my shirt was now flapping loosely and a thin line of blood accentuated the horizontal swipe the blade had made. It wasn't a deep cut, but I had a feeling "Mom" had lost all interest in chopping on that tenderloin. Jori's cry seemed to halt the attack on me for a moment. Another shudder. Then, "Mom" turned and began advancing on *Jori.*

I picked up a wooden chair, held it by its back, and swung it full force. The base of the chair connected with the side of "Mom's" head at what should have been terminal velocity. The meat cleaver flew harmlessly to the floor and skidded across the room. Her head whipped to the left, and she moved in a halting, discombobulated walk to the counter where she steadied herself. I gaped in disbelief. She should have been plastered to the floor – maybe dead from the force of that blow.

Troy would have suggested lightening things up a bit at this point, so I looked across the room to Jori and motioned toward "Mom" with an incline of my head. "She didn't use to be so *moody.* I have a feeling somebody gave her an attitude adjustment while I was away." Keeping a wary eye on "Mom" – who remained immobile at the counter, Jori crossed the kitchen. I positioned her behind me in what I knew to be a very heroic gesture based on all of the movies that I had ever seen. In real life, however, when people are trying to play butcher shop with *you* as the choice cut of meat, it quickly becomes clear how totally overrated the whole hero thing truly is.

Suddenly, "Mom" seemed to feel the need to reiterate some of her earlier words of motherly advice. She jerked her head into an upright position and let loose with several rounds of, "You're supposed to tell your family if you're leaving the house. *Everyone knows that.*" She proceeded to repeat this phrase over and over again. Simultaneously, she turned her head to the left as if sharing her words with an assembled crowd and then to the right to be sure that we heard her as well. It was when she looked toward us for the first time, that Jori blew out my eardrums.

"AAAAAAAAHHHHH! *Oh, no! Oh, NO!* It can't be! Jack, she's not . . . She's . . .What *is* it?"

My jaw hung open. This woman. The impostor. Dear old "Mom," as I liked to refer to her, was not a woman at all. The skin on the right side of her face, where the chair had collided with her, was scrunched up in a huge wad directly above her right eye. It was a nauseating sight in and of itself, but what lay underneath was even more horrific – a mass of circuitry, wires, and blinking lights. "Mom" was a machine!

Chapter Eighteen

Neither Jori nor I felt like hanging around in the kitchen after our guest appearance in "Mom's" killer cafe movie. Besides, if she decided to try her meat cleaver scene again, I'd have preferred she looked elsewhere for a co-star. My impression was that she wasn't much of a threat anymore, but why stick around to find out? As we made our way into the living room, which was eerily silent, I reminded myself that there could be more "Moms" somewhere just waiting to attack. At this point, anything was possible. If he'd created one artificial mother, couldn't he have made two or three? Jori parked Gram's makeup bag on the coffee table, opened it, and began rummaging around. I attempted to peer over her shoulder – neither Troy nor I had ever had a chance to see what all was in there – but she shoved me down onto the sofa.

"Sit down for a second. We need to take care of that cut. Hey, here's just what we need." She removed a tube of ointment and some of those "baby wipe" cloths from the bag.

"I swear that bag of hers is a bottomless supply pit!" I said.

"It's not entirely bottomless. I can't find any gauze or tape to patch you up with." Jori tossed me some of the damp cloths and the ointment. "Here. Wash off some of the blood and spread this ointment on."

I ripped away the large flap of my shirt that was hanging down and followed her instructions. Then, I tossed the ointment back to her and placed the bloodied cloths in the ashtray – a small act of defiance, but I enjoyed it. The bleeding had been minor, but there was a clear line of incision across the middle of my chest. When I looked at it, I felt kind of sick. "Okay." I stood up. "He has to know we're here, and he knows we're going to be looking for Gram and Troy. He's probably watching us this very minute, but there's nothing we can do. The question is where do we look for them?"

"But Jack, if he knows where we are, why is he waiting? Why doesn't he come and face us himself? You said he was going to be expecting you."

"I don't know. Maybe I'm wrong about him knowing where we are. Maybe he isn't here. He said he had to *secure* Troy. I'm not sure what that means, but it doesn't sound like something that would be easily accomplished knowing my brother. Maybe that's taken Dad longer than he thought it would. I'm not sure that he found Gram either; he was kind of vague on that issue when he was arguing with himself back at the house. Maybe Gram and Troy have kept him so busy, he hasn't had time to prepare for me."

She moved softly to the piano and studied the pictures that were displayed on the closed lid. "This is interesting. A picture of Mr. Eden, I mean . . . your father, with your mother. And here's one of him with your grandmother. And then these two frames are empty."

"Huh?" I walked over to the piano. I had never seen these pictures or the frames before. Jori was right – there were four 5X7 frames resting on the piano lid. The first contained a photo of my father and mother – actually it was of my father and the impostor. I could tell because of the "Mrs. America" wardrobe – the dress was far too flashy, even for a portrait. My mother had better taste. The second photo was of Dad and Gram. Two additional frames that matched the others perfectly were empty. My eyes strayed back to the photo of Dad and Gram. As I was wondering when that picture had been taken and why I'd never seen it before, a noise from the second floor caught my attention. "Did you hear that?" It was clear from Jori's expression that she had heard it, too. She moved quickly to my side and clasped my hand. I began leading us cautiously toward the stairs when she suddenly dropped my hand, wheeled around, and headed back to the coffee table for the makeup bag.

"You never know!" she said as she smiled and reunited with me.

"You're right. You *never* know," I said flashing her a grin. I really liked this girl. She was smart, bold, and beautiful – a lethal combination.

We made our way up the stairs, and the sound grew louder. It seemed to be a knocking or banging of some kind. As we headed down the hall, we noticed it was coming from my grandmother's room. We sped up.

"Jack, it sounds like someone's beating on a door."

She was right. That's exactly what it sounded like. We headed into Gram's room through her open bedroom door. The commotion was coming from her closet. I didn't even hesitate. I dropped Jori's hand and surveyed the door. Chain locks had been placed at the top and bottom of the door, and both were positioned to secure it. I reached up to release them. "Gram? Gram, is it you?" The moment they were unlatched I yanked on the knob, and my grandmother, who had been leaning against the door on her knees, tumbled out of the darkened closet.

"Gram!"

"Mrs. Barrett!"

Both Jori and I were aghast at her condition. She appeared very weak and was clearly unsteady. We helped her to the bed to sit.

"Jack, oh Jackie, thank the good Lord you heard me." She put her arms around me and pulled me to her. I held her for a long time hoping that she would draw strength from the knowledge that she was no longer alone.

"It's going to be okay, Gram. I'm here now. We're going to find Troy and get out of here." She squeezed my hand affectionately, and then she officially noticed Jori. The fact that she remembered my girlfriend's name delighted me.

"Jori, darling." She took Jori's hand and clasped it in
hers as Jori sat beside her on the bed. "Thank you for
helping him. You must have. Am I right?"

Jori blushed. "It didn't take much convincing, Mrs.
Barrett." She looked at me, and her eyes sparkled.

Gram's voice didn't seem to have its usual zesty
power, but she mustered a somewhat perky response.
"Now let's drop the whole *Mrs. Barrett* thing right here
and now. I'm Gram to him, and I'm Gram to you.
Agreed?"

I grinned at my grandmother in appreciation.

"Agreed, Mrs. Barre . . . I mean, Gram."

Just then Gram seemed to notice my upper apparel or
lack thereof. When I ripped away the section of my shirt
that was under the slicing line, it didn't leave a whole lot.
"Jack, sweetheart, explain to your grandmother why you
feel the need to wear only the top half of your shirt. I'm
up on all the fashion trends, and this isn't one of them.
You've obviously got the girl already so there's no need
to go around showing off . . ."

"Gram!" I was blushing big time. "This happened
downstairs in the kitchen." Jori shot me a warning look
and shook her head very slowly. She didn't want me to
talk about what had happened downstairs. Probably a
good idea. "I . . . uh . . . I . . . got my shirt caught in the
garbage disposal. Yeah, *the garbage disposal*, that's it."

"The garbage disposal!" She looked at me
incredulously. "Jack, go sell that story somewhere else.

Why don't you just tell me that you don't *want* to tell me
because you're afraid you'll upset me?"

You can't get anything by my grandmother. Looking
back now, the garbage disposal was a pretty lame story; *I*
wouldn't even have believed me. "All right, Gram, since
you suggested it – I *don't* want to tell you because I *am*
afraid it will upset you."

"*Oh, hogwash*! Don't you ever say such a thing to
me again. I'm not some old woman who needs protection
from the truth. Now, out with it!"

Jori and I both grinned. "Jori, you are now officially
meeting my grandmother. She's impossible!" We both
laughed, and Gram smiled warmly. Her smile reminded
me of the one in the photo of her with Dad on the piano.
Again, my mind returned to those photos. Why had he set
up all four frames ahead of time like that when he only
had the two photos? And when did he get Gram to pose
for a picture with him? Surely not since we'd moved
here. Yet the photo looked so recent. I was puzzled and
decided to ask Gram about it, but Jori had a surprise to
reveal.

"Oh, by the way Mrs. . . ." Gram cautioned her with a
finger, and Jori corrected herself. "I mean, Gram. I have
something for you." Jori moved to retrieve the makeup
bag that she'd left sitting beside the bedroom door. I was
anxious to witness Gram's jubilation upon being reunited
with it. I expected her to be thrilled, but I sensed that
something was wrong before Jori even had her hands on
the bag. Gram's eyes were following her to it, as were

mine, but there was no comment. No joyous moment of
recognition, no gasp of amazement. *Nothing.* Jori lifted
the bag and headed back to the bed.

At last Gram spoke. "What is it, Dear? Is there a
surprise in your bag for me?"

A moment of terribly awkward silence followed.
Either Jori or I should have responded with some kind of
fake casual conversation immediately to protect our
discovery, but we were both too stunned to speak.
Obviously, the silence made it clear that we knew. Upon
hearing Gram's comment, Jori had stopped abruptly and
moved no closer to her. Unfortunately, I was seated on
the bed beside her. I made a careful move to distance
myself, but her hand shot out and grabbed my throat in a
grip like a steel vise. She then placed the other arm
around my chest and drew me up against her so tightly
that I literally couldn't move my arms. It was as if they
were barred by lead. She was incredibly strong –
inhumanly strong.

"Please." Jori pleaded. "Don't do this. Whoever you
are, *whatever* you are. Don't . . ." she took a step towards
us.

Groping fingers began to create cavities in my neck. I
winced in pain, and a struggle for air was underway.
Then, she spoke. Her voice was Gram's, but it wasn't.
There was an absence of all the things that truly made my
grandmother who she was in the voice of this creature.
"I'm going to crush his windpipe."

Chapter Nineteen

My arms and legs began to kick frantically as it became harder and harder to breathe, but it was no use. It was clear that I was caught in a "death grip" – literally, and that the panicked and helpless expression on Jori's face would be my final glimpse of her. What had I gotten her into? And then another thought struck me – one that bothered me much more than the fact that oxygen and I were quickly becoming strangers. What were they going to do to her when I was gone? That thought, the idea that they would hurt her, maybe even kill her, renewed my strength, and I began to fight with everything I had left. I've heard that you can tell when you truly love someone because in times of crisis your own welfare is no longer your primary concern. At that moment, I realized just how true the adage is.

Jori stood there helplessly and began to beg one last time for my release. She extended her hands imploringly to this creature that was sucking the life out of me. "*Please* . . . please stop this!" The fake "grandmother" disregarded her completely and pressed even more forcefully against my throat to take the rest of the fight out of me. Jori then tried to contact a new source for help. It seemed almost laughable to me, but I guess when you're desperate you'll turn to anyone for help. "Mr. Eden? Mr. Barrett?" She looked toward the open door and called out to him. "Are you here somewhere? Do you *know* what is happening? Please! He's your *son*! Won't you help him? There's still time to . . ."

"Let go of my grandson, or I'll turn you into a trash compactor!" My vision was growing somewhat blurry, but there was no mistaking the voice. *Gram*, the real Gram, had arrived. She sprang into the doorway holding a . . . what did she have in her hand? It almost looked like a . . . no, surely not. All at once, a mini-tidal wave was headed straight in my direction. I dropped my chin as much as the "death-grip" would allow, and it was just enough. The main stream of water sailed just above my head and struck my captor squarely in the face. The hands around my neck were immediately withdrawn in an effort to block the steady stream of water. I stumbled forward and fell on all fours gasping for air. Jori moved toward me, but Gram called to her.

"Jori! Here, cover me, honey!" My vision had cleared enough at this point to confirm what I had earlier doubted. As I watched, my grandmother kept one weapon trained and firing on her phony double while tossing Jori another one of my brother's *Super Squirts*. The plastic guns shot water in a hard spray from distances of up to twelve feet and, when they had their emergency tanks connected and filled, the stream could continue for up to one minute. One minute is a lot of time when you're being bombarded with water. I know. Troy had to have someone to practice on in order to become the only kid on our block who could fire two guns simultaneously with pinpoint accuracy. Just as Gram's water supply began to dwindle, Jori started up. The power of the stream was in no way equal to the strength in the hands that had grasped my throat with such force, but it was clearly serving as a source of confusion. And, if I knew Gram, it wouldn't take long for her to put this machine out of order. I had to assume this was a machine similar to the one downstairs – although clearly this one had been a more convincing replacement. Dad must have improved on some of the problems with "Mom" before putting this model into operation.

As Jori's gun dispensed its artillery, Gram ran to her makeup bag. I was just getting to my feet and beginning to feel some control over my breathing again, and I watched in fascination as Gram began pulling long cords from her bag. It looked to be far more cord than could ever fit inside, and I marveled at her packing job. Then, she pulled out the clamps. *Jumper cables*! What was she doing with jumper cables in there? She tossed one end towards me.

"Jack, sweetheart, be a dear and clamp those onto my twin sister over there. I'm about to become an only child." She then produced an electric drill which she used to remove the cover from one of the electrical outlets on the wall.

I tentatively approached Gram's "twin." The water was ricocheting off of her and onto me as I handed over

the two ends of the cables. "Here, hold these a minute.
Would you?" Surprisingly, she grasped them with both
hands as I backed away quickly, and Gram, wearing
insulated gloves, clamped the other end of the cables to
the screw terminals inside the outlet. The effects were
immediate and spectacular. Gram's "twin" began a
pronounced and clearly involuntary series of jerks, and
we could literally see the electricity passing through her.
Then, there was smoke and, for a moment, a dazzling
display of sparks. The machine then crumpled to the
ground.

I looked over and there stood Gram with a *sparkler* in
her hand – the kind kids like to hold on July 4th during
the fireworks. She was waving it through the air and
making designs just like I used to do when I was little. I
shook my head in disbelief, but she pretended she didn't
understand. "What? I wanted to do something to
commemorate her short but influential life. It's a shame
really," she said with fake sincerity. "She had such
potential!" She reached into her makeup bag and pulled
out two more sparklers. "You guys want these?"

At the conclusion of Gram's fireworks, we began to
search the entire second floor for signs of Troy. We also
used the time to trade stories about what had gone on
during my absence from Paradise. Gram seemed
somewhat prepared for the news about Mom – maybe
because she'd been gone for so long, but I don't think she
ever considered for a minute that it was actually my father
who had killed her. Then, I had to break the bigger news.

To say that she was shaken to discover that her son and Mr. Eden were one and the same would be an understatement. She stopped in the hallway and placed one hand against the wall to steady herself. "*No*. Jack, how could it be? *Two men in the same body?* How can you be sure? Why, this would mean that Chip is . . ."

"Insane, Gram." I finished her sentence. "Some people might call it a multiple personality disorder, but when you're building androids to replace living people, electrically fencing in villages, and murdering your family, I'd say we need to go with insanity as the first level of diagnosis." My attempt to lighten the mood seemed lost on her for the moment.

Jori put a hand on Gram's shoulder. "I'm sorry, Mrs. Barrett."

"Call me Gram, honey. They all do." She looked away from both of us. When she turned back, her eyes were moist. "Did I do this? Did I *cause* this in some way?" Gram looked at me. "I'm his *mother*, Jack. I knew that something was wrong. I could see that he needed help. He was always so *obsessed* with perfection. Everything had to be perfect – his room, his clothes, his grades, his friends, his . . . parents." She put her hands to the sides of her face, and the tears flowed freely. "But we *weren't*. Never. From the time he was in his early teens, he criticized us both relentlessly. And friends, oh my, he couldn't keep friends because he was constantly finding fault with them. He was ruthless, Jack, so hurtful. I'm not talking about typical teenage rebellion, either. Chip was *cruel*."

"Gram, I didn't know. You never told us anything about . . ."

"Amos and I went to counseling, but Chip wouldn't go. He wouldn't talk to anyone about it. Oh, we tried everything. We punished him in ways the counselor suggested. We rewarded him for the slightest display of compassion toward anyone! We *tried* to talk with him, but nothing worked."

"But all these years, you never said anything."

"We agreed never to say anything to you boys or your mother about it. We didn't want to cause more problems, and it seemed that Chip was better when he met Susan. Your mother had a way of *softening* his harshness. Amos used to say she could melt him with one look. We never heard him express disapproval of her – at least not until this business with Eden started, and by then your grandfather was gone, thank goodness. Chip was a good father to you, his first-born, and so very proud of you. And then Troy was born, and for some reason there was an instant connection. I've never understood why, but your father seemed to feel that Troy was better than the average child. He saw Troy as *exceptional* in every category."

"But, Gram, if that were true, then why didn't I ever feel any comparison? Dad never gave me the impression that he liked Troy better than me."

"Oh, Jack, he never would have said anything in front of you, but he told everyone else. It wasn't that he liked Troy better. He didn't see it as a comparison, darling, because in his view no one *could* compare with Troy. It simply was impossible. But when your brother began rebelling against Chip's efforts to control him, he became the object of your father's disdain." She paused, and I could tell she was going to reveal something else I didn't know. "Jack, when your grandfather and I moved into the house, it *was* because we wanted to be closer to you boys, but it was *also* because of Troy. We began seeing signs of your father's old behaviors when we would visit. Chip was terribly hard on your brother, and we were worried that Troy might need someone looking out for him. Your mother had never seen that side of Chip, and we weren't sure if she'd be able to handle it. She did her best, but it took all of us to shield Troy from what eventually became a consistent battery of verbal criticism. Chip seemed to become irritated with your brother at the slightest sign of imperfection."

"Poor Troy. How terrible for him to feel so pressured." Jori was obviously being pulled into the story as much as I was.

Gram looked down at the floor and nodded in agreement. She addressed Jori, then, as she began relating a story that I had never heard. "I remember one afternoon I went with Troy and Chip to the park while Susan and Amos took Jack to some kind of scouting event. Chip rented a big bucket of baseballs, and I sat and watched as he pitched them to Troy. Troy was only a little squirt, but he hit eight out of the first ten balls his father pitched. Well, Chip walked over to him, knelt down, and explained that although he was doing a good job, he needed to try *harder* to hit all ten balls. Troy nodded and eagerly positioned his bat for another series of pitches." Her face took on a forlorn expression, our eyes met, and suddenly I became her target audience. "Jack, he missed the very next ball, and your father exploded – yelling at him and telling him he was *worthless*! I tried to intervene, but Chip ignored me. He started pitching again, and little Troy was so nervous, so terribly nervous. I could see it."

"What happened, Gram?" I had to know how this ended. It could explain a lot of things about my brother.

"Well, Troy managed to hit the next few balls your father pitched, but then Chip began throwing them faster and harder. It was evident to me that with every moment of Troy's success, your father was raising the bar higher. Finally, he pitched a curve ball . . . a *curve* ball – to a little eight-year-old! Troy didn't even come close to hitting it. How could he? And then your father . . . he just went wild. I'd never seen him like that. He . . . he began throwing the balls *at* Troy. Hard."

Gram grimaced as she related the story; it was obviously very painful for her to relive these dark moments from the past. "Chip began screaming at Troy and telling him that he was never going to be anything if he couldn't learn to strive for perfection – that he had all of the potential but none of the ambition. It was ridiculous. Troy couldn't even have understood what any of that meant at his age. And Chip was bombarding him with the balls. Jack, he was *trying* to hit him, and he succeeded several times before I was able to stop him. Little Troy just stood there with tears running down his dirt-stained cheeks, pleading with his father to stop." She paused and brought her hands to her chest. "Your brother was never the same after that. Pleasing your father never mattered to him anymore."

Jori was outraged. "What kind of man would do that to his own little boy? I can't believe he wasn't arrested or something."

"He did come to his senses later in the day and apologized to Troy, but it was too late. After that, Troy never wanted to be alone with Chip, and we made sure that he wasn't," Gram said.

Lots of things about my brother's rebellious attitude were making sense all of a sudden. What I couldn't believe was that he had never told me about any of this. We shared everything with one another, or so I thought. This was big stuff to keep from me, but I had a feeling I knew why. How could he tell me without making it sound as though I was the "less-than-perfect" brother? I'm okay with who I am. I'm good at lots of things, and I'm not jealous of my brother's charms and talents – most of the time, but I could see how it would be hard for him to tell me *this* story. Gram looked so sad by the end of the tale that I felt a need to change the subject. As we entered Troy's room and began scouring it for clues, I asked her how she had come into possession of my brother's two "Super Squirts."

She threw back her head and laughed. "That little devil! Jack, he came to check on me after dinner last night and insisted I leave my room and go into hiding. I was still feeling pretty shaky and had no intention of getting out of bed, but your brother can be very persuasive. He refused to tell me when you were coming back – in fact, he refused to give me any information whatsoever until I agreed to let him hide me. Well, before I knew it, my new address was the back half of a bathtub. He gave me a stool to sit on, pulled the shower curtain halfway across the tub, and announced that I was perfectly hidden."

"What did he expect you to do?" Jori asked. We were both giggling at the image of my grandmother sitting on a stool in the back end of a bathtub.

"That's what *I* asked him. And do you know what he told me?"

"What?" I could hardly wait to hear this.

"He said I should just wait patiently for someone to come and tell me that the coast was clear. He also left me some supplies that were meant, I suppose, to keep me from becoming bored."

"Supplies?" Jori questioned. "What kind of supplies?"

"Honey, don't ever take Troy with you on a survival trip. His supply bag included a pile of magazines with pictures of T.V.'s hottest teen girls, two boxes of stale lemon candies, a walkman that played music with words I couldn't recognize, and those two loaded squirt guns! Then, he refused to tell me anything about what had happened since my little shock treatment until I *promised* to stay in the bathtub."

"And you did?" I couldn't believe she'd given in to him.

"I had no choice! I needed the scoop, Jack. I'd been out of the loop for several hours." She looked at Jori and winked conspiratorially. "We girls *hate* being out of the loop!"

Jori nodded. "You know it, Gram!"

My grandmother beamed and patted Jori's hand to show that she was pleased she had not been called "Mrs. Barrett." Then, she continued her story at a rapid pace. "Anyway, when I heard my *own* voice coming from down the hall, I began wondering if that electric jolt had fried my gray matter. But then I heard your voices, and from the sound of things you needed a hand. Promise or no promise, I had to do something. Whoever would have thought those crazy water guns of his would have actually come in handy?"

"Troy would have thought so!" Jori and I spoke in unison and smiled at each other. It was funny how quickly she was coming to know my brother. She'd only met him once, but from all of my stories and now Gram's, too, she obviously had him pegged.

We found nothing in Troy's room and headed
downstairs in search of clues to his whereabouts. The
three of us combed my father's study first. It's frustrating
when you're looking so diligently for something, but you
don't actually know what it is that you're looking for. As
we hunted, I gave Gram the news about her old friend,
Bill Simpson, but she remained steadfast in her belief that
he would not have betrayed her. "He must have been
another one of these robots or androids, or whatever you
call them." Her eyes developed a sadness then. "Bill
didn't ever have much in the way of family. To hear him
talk, Amos and I *were* his family. Why, just a couple of
years ago I stood with him at the wake for his Aunt Sarah,
and at the end of the evening he said, 'Well, Katie, she
was the last one. You're all I have left in the way of
family now.' No, Bill would *never* betray me, Jack. He
just wouldn't."

"But Gram," I countered, "if he was an android –
programmed by Dad, why would he have told me all of
that stuff about the sale of the stock. You said yourself
that story all made sense."

"Maybe," Jori jumped in, "Mr. Simpson was the
earliest model, and he was programmed with *all* of the
original Mr. Simpson's knowledge. You said your
mother's replacement had *some* of her knowledge, but
other things about her seemed to have been altered like
the way she dressed and the way she spoke. Maybe your
father didn't begin altering the androids until *after* Mr.
Simpson was replaced."

"There you go. Smart girl you've got there, Jack. That's just the explanation I was going to suggest!" Gram winked at Jori, squeezed her hand, and whispered loudly enough so I could hear her. "Stick close, sweetheart. I may need you again."

"Okay you two – let's remember we're a threesome here. And we're about to be a foursome." The stories about my little brother were having a tremendous emotional pull on me. I closed the last desk drawer. "There's nothing here. He has Troy. I know he does, and I know where we need to go – follow me." I headed for the basement door and, for some reason, this time I wasn't thinking so much about how I hated being underground. Instead, I was remembering the dream I'd had – the one where Troy was calling out for me to save him while Mr. Eden's office at The Garden School was filling up with poisonous gas. Somehow, it felt like he was calling out to me now. I hadn't been able to save him in the dream, but I was going to save him now – or die trying.

Chapter Twenty

As we headed down the basement stairs, I felt confident that my father was waiting for us; I also couldn't shake the notion that we might be underground for a very long time. We arrived at the closet first. I expected the hat and coat to be in their usual place, but they were missing. Two empty hooks. The real question: Was that good or bad? I didn't really know.

"Jack?" Jori's voice was quiet and cautious as she motioned with her head toward the other door. It was *open*. "What's in there? Look at all of these bolts and locks on the door!"

I was looking at the other side of the door for the first time. "Well, the big secret's over. He obviously wants us to know," I said. Then, a funny thought struck me as I prepared to enter the room. When I watch a horror movie, I'm always saying how stupid the heroes are for going into rooms just like this one, and here I was leading the way! I decided to go easier on those movie heroes in the future.

As we entered the room, small lamps along the walls began to slowly illuminate the darkness. The first thing I noticed was two benches about four feet long, one on each side of the room, and two poles placed approximately two feet from the benches on each side. The room also contained a long narrow table that was bolted to the floor and situated perpendicular to the ends of the benches. I looked the table over carefully. There were some kind of metal restraints attached to it. The largest was designed to swing out and lock over a person's chest while the other four were positioned to secure wrists and ankles. *Troy had been on this table.* I felt sure of it, and my blood began to boil. What had they done to him? What were they doing to him right now?

"Jack, are these *windows*?" Jori's gentle voice broke into my thoughts. She and Gram were clicking their nails against a hard plastic surface that was lining the walls. The lights remained dim, and I was about to suggest we look for a way to turn them up when we heard the sound of compressed air as the door closed forcefully. We watched as all of the locks clicked into place mechanically. Then, the lights became quite brilliant, and we were jolted forward. All three of us grabbed instinctively for the poles. The "room" was moving. The soft hum of an engine could barely be heard as we gained momentum with each passing second.

"What the . . ." I could barely contain my astonishment. "This isn't a room! It's some kind of a *tram*."

"Oh, dear Lord," Gram said. "These theme park rides always upset my stomach. Jori, honey, open my makeup bag and get me some antacid pills. There's some licorice in there if you kids are hungry."

"No thanks, Gram." I smiled at her affectionately. Jori, who was becoming quite adept with Gram's bag, found the pills rather easily and pulled out a container of bottled water as well.

"Here, Gram," she said. "You'll need something to wash those pills down with – right?"

My grandmother nodded appreciatively, took the pills and water, and downed them quickly.

"Any guesses where we're going?" I asked them.

"How about your father's office at the school?" Jori suggested. "You said it was deep underground. Maybe it's connected to your house."

I considered that for a minute but then discounted it. "No, I don't think he'd take us to the school; it isn't isolated enough. I wonder if . . ."

"*Eden.*" Gram didn't just offer it as a suggestion – she proclaimed it. "He's taking us to the corporate headquarters. Remember how he talked about it when we first drove into town, Jack. He's the CEO. That's where he feels the most powerful. He wants us on his turf and on his terms."

We both agreed that she was correct. It all made sense. Without warning the tram slowed and then, rather suddenly, it began a steady ascent. The change in course brought me two conflicting sensations. The fact that we were going above ground eased the queasiness in my stomach, but the thought that we were undoubtedly about to confront my father returned me to my nauseous state.

Sensing we were nearing the end of our ride, Gram began to speak quickly. "We have one thing going for us, kids," she said. "I don't think Chip is used to being resisted – at least not as Mr. Eden, and I don't think Mr. Eden has a great deal of experience coping with human beings who can think independently. The more I think about our experiences with the people in this village, the more I think that they're *all* androids. They obey his every command. They're *too* happy. *Too* content. They can't be real."

Of course! Gram's words made it all crystal clear to me. I simply hadn't stopped to think about it before. The whole village! All the people on the streets downtown. The kids at The Garden School. Old Cora who took Troy for the elevator ride. The girl Gram had spoken to at the government office. All androids. *None of them were real.* I shuddered. "Well, if we're going to be facing androids, we're going to need some weapons," I said. There was absolutely nothing in the tram which could be of any use to us, so Gram began rummaging through her makeup bag.

"Ugghh!" She grunted, and we heard the sound of the contents of her bag being jostled about as she pulled an iron rod out and proceeded to *unfold* it. Both Jori and I stared at her in disbelief. "What?" she asked innocently. "It's a *collapsible* tire iron. You never know when you might need one, and here we are in just that type of situation! And to think I almost passed this little baby up on the Home Shopping Network! Here, Jack. You keep

this with you." I took the rod eagerly. It felt good to have
something heavy in my hand even if I didn't really want
to use it.

The tram stopped. We heard the sound of compressed
air again, and the latches on the door were released. It
opened. We peered carefully through the doorway and
there, at the far end of a long but narrow room, we saw
him waiting for us. My father – *Mr. Eden.*

He was sitting at a large desk, and his hat and coat
were in place as always. I knew he'd left a hat and coat in
the closet back in Davenport so I considered a
conversation starter focusing on how many sets of
matching outerwear he owned, but then another thought
struck me. Why did he continue to pull the brim of the
hat down and turn the coat collar up? His identity was no
longer a secret to us. Surely, he knew that. And then it
hit me. *We* knew that he was really two people, but did
he know? He'd interrupted Jori at the gatehouse,
seemingly to protect his dual identity, but had that been a
conscious decision he'd made or some kind of bizarre
psychological safety mechanism that had happened
without his knowledge?

As we stepped out into the room, the door hissed shut.
I was prepared for the tram to leave, but it remained
stationary. I wondered what replaced it when it *did* leave.
Was there some kind of mechanical wall that slid down
from the ceiling? Was there an invisible force field that
provided closure to this part of the room when the tram
was gone? I supposed anything was possible in this

place. We advanced cautiously across an impressive tiled floor that contained an intricate pattern that was woven throughout the room's outer edges. A few steps ahead of us there was a small "living room" ensemble – an inviting sofa, armchair, coffee table, and lamp were all positioned on a luxurious rug and looked as though they had never been used. We slowed our pace just past the furniture grouping and stared at him. The moonlight creeping through the tall arched windows behind his desk created a bizarre aura of light behind him. He stood and beckoned us forward with his finger. "Jack. Mrs. Barrett. Welcome to *Eden*." His voice was hushed, but the word *Eden* had been pronounced very forcefully and with unmistakable pride.

All three of us stopped simultaneously when he spoke. A long and awkward pause followed. I don't think any of us knew what to say. Based on his decision to address Gram as "Mrs. Barrett," I assumed that he was truly unaware of the fact that he was not only Mr. Eden but also her son, Chip Barrett. I wondered if, for the moment, addressing him as Mr. Eden and not as my father was the safest route for all of us; yet, I was also tempted by the idea of breaking the news to him that he was a lunatic. Jori, who had been completely ignored during his greeting, stalled my decision when she began to introduce herself.

"I'm Jori," she said in a tone that was neither friendly nor hostile. "You probably didn't recognize me since you've only seen me at the gate . . ."

"There's someone I'm sure you're *both* eager to see."
He appeared to be addressing only Gram and me as he
spoke. He made no response to Jori's attempt to greet
him. In fact, he seemed completely dismissive of her. He
reached toward a panel on his desk that contained several
buttons and pressed one. A door hidden in the front wall
of his office opened, and *Troy* came racing into the room.

"Gram!" He flung his arms around her waist.
"You're all right!"

She looked at me. We were both thinking the same
thing – this was probably another android. Yet, we
couldn't be sure. We would have to wait for a sign.
Gram embraced him.

"Troy, you little devil, I was worried sick about you!
I'm glad to see you're all right!"

"Hey, little bro," I said. "Long time no see, huh?"

"Jack! Man, are you a sight for sore eyes." He gave
me a quick hug. "What's with the shirt? You headin' for
the beach or something? Or maybe just trying to look
good for this *fine lady* here." He was looking at Jori. If
he acted like he'd never met her, then I'd know. I readied
the rod in my hand. "Obviously you and my big brother
have quite the romance going . . ." I relaxed my grip on
the rod. "But if you ever get tired of him and want to
hang out with a guy who's all about excitement, I'd be
pleased to step in. Back in Davenport, the girls called me
the *love doctor*."

I brought the rod down and swept his right leg hard
and fast. He screamed in pain and grabbed for the injured

leg as he fell. Troy might flirt with a girl we were both meeting for the first time, but he would never behave this way in front of a girl who was special to me. I steeled myself for the sight of blinking circuits and wiring.

"Jack?" Gram's voice registered astonishment as she and Jori moved to help Troy. I looked down and, to my surprise, I saw blood flowing freely from a huge gash that I'd just created in his leg. He was rocking on the floor and biting his lip to hold back the tears. I was dumbstruck. I let the rod fall and the sound of it clanking against the floor tiles echoed through the room. I looked at my father. He was just standing there – not saying a word. Simply staring at all of us.

"*What did you do to him?*" I was startled by the sound of my own voice as I approached the desk. I couldn't see them, but I knew Gram's and Jori's eyes were following me.

He remained completely calm as he spoke. "*I* didn't do anything to him. *You* seem to have wounded him. Pity. He'll recover, though this little escapade doesn't say much for *brotherly love,* now does it?"

Jori was by my side in a moment. "Love? What do you know about love? Any man who would . . ."

"Jori!" I cut her off. I was afraid that in a rush of anger she would bring his dual personality to light, and I wasn't ready to play our hand just yet. I redirected the conversation. "He *isn't* my brother. At least not the way he used to be. Troy would *never* have hit on my girl that way. What did you do to him?"

He put his finger to his chin. "Aaaahhh, yes, the *girl*." He looked at Jori with contempt. "*You've* become quite a problem. I instructed Jack's father to make it clear that you weren't allowed in the village. It would seem he wasn't an *effective* communicator." He reached toward another panel on his desk and held his finger suspended over one of the buttons. Then he brought his face up out of the collar, just a bit, and I saw it twist into a scornful grimace. "*I*, on the other hand, am a *most* effective communicator. So understand me when I say – you *don't* belong here." He pressed the button then, and I was instantly thrown clear of Jori by some kind of powerful force. The air around her began to crackle with energy, and she was immersed in what looked like a field of electricity. Little pieces of lightning seemed to be coursing through and around her body, and she released an agonizing scream – long and sustained – that cut into my heart like a jagged knife. Then her body began to twist and writhe as if she were in some kind of slow motion torture chamber. I jumped to my feet and began to move toward her, but Troy grabbed my ankle.

"*Don't*. He might make it worse if you defy him." His eyes made it clear to me that he was truly concerned about Jori's safety.

"Troy! *Compassion*? I thought we'd gotten rid of all that." He seemed quite amazed by Troy's comment. Not angry, simply puzzled. He released the button, and Jori crumpled to the floor. All three of us moved toward her, but the tapping of his finger on the desk held us in check.

"Ah, ah, ah! No closer please, or I shall be forced to resume my little demonstration."

At that point, Gram took charge. "Chip Barrett . . ."

"Gram!" I was desperate for her to keep quiet, but she was too far gone. She stormed around the desk and moved right into his face.

"You'd better pray that girl is all right, Chip. Wasn't *Susan's* death enough to satisfy your appetite for a while?" A shudder ran through him at the mention of my mother's name. I don't think Gram even noticed it. Once she spoke Mom's name aloud, it seemed to trigger something inside of her. Everything she'd been holding back was released, and she began verbally assaulting him with everything she could muster. "How did you do it, Chip? How did you *kill* Susan?" There. The shudder again. Maybe Gram *did* notice because my mother became the artillery in the attack. "She loved you, Chip. *Susan.* Your wife loved you, but you killed her – *didn't you?*" He began backing away from Gram, but she pursued. "Why?" She choked back a sob as she continued her barrage. "Because she wasn't *perfect*? Didn't she fit in here? Couldn't you *make* her fit in? What went wrong? Why did you have to kill her? Why did you *kill* your own wife?"

What happened to my father's face and body at that moment defies description. It was unlike anything I had ever seen, and I hope I never witness anything like it again. He began to alter – physically. It began with his head which started to turn slowly from side to side as his facial muscles twitched and pulsed simultaneously. The pupils of his eyes became huge. Then, they grew smaller as his jaw seemed to realign itself. The coat fell effortlessly to the floor, and he flipped the hat away as he brought both of his arms up to hide his face from our view. But it was too late; we'd already seen it. His entire body became tremulous – like he was having a mild seizure, and then, all at once, he was still.

"Dear God in heaven!" My grandmother brought her hand to her mouth and backed away from him slowly just as he brought his arms down.

"You!" He spat the word at her. "I might have known you'd succeed in creating more problems for me, Mother. Well, it couldn't matter less this time because you're too late. *Mr. Eden* will take care of you this time. *All of you.*" He swung his eyes around to where I was now helping Jori to sit up. She had some sort of strange burn marks all over her skin, and she winced when I touched her arms.

"Even *me*?" Troy stood gingerly. He reached for the edge of the desk and leaned against it. I had obviously done quite a number on his leg.

"What?" My father was clearly astonished that Troy was in the room. But why was that so amazing to him? "How did you get . . ." Then, all at once, his eyes grew wide, and he began to gape at Troy in childlike wonder. He gasped and raced around the desk. "Adam *did it*! *You're here!*" He grabbed Troy's shoulders and his jubilance was unrestrained. "You're *really* here. You're complete! For a minute I thought that you were . . ." He stopped as he suddenly became aware that we were staring at him.

By this time, I had decided it was time for us to scram before something happened to trigger Mr. Eden's return. I looked at Gram and Jori to cue them and then delivered a very casual line that I didn't think had a prayer of truly getting us safely out. Still, it was the best that I could think of at the time. "Well, now that we've found Troy, we'll head on back to the house, Dad." I took Troy's arm somewhat firmly to pull him away from my father and toward the door of the tram, which I had no idea how to open, but he hesitated for a moment – just long enough for me to know that he wasn't sure he was going to leave. What had happened to my brother? Was he afraid to leave? Didn't he *want* to leave?

"You're not taking *him* anywhere. He belongs to Adam now. He's Adam's *son*. The *perfect* son."

I released my grip and bent down to grab the tire iron. "Look," I said slamming one end of the weapon into the palm of my other hand. I was trying to look as threatening as I could. "We've had enough of all this. We're leaving now. *All* of us. I don't want to use this, Dad, but I will if you force me. Now step away from Troy." He did as I asked.

"Troy, honey, come on." Gram had stepped up and was directing Troy away from my father. It seemed to me that Troy was very tentative though – still uncertain about something. I turned to Jori.

"You okay?"

"My skin feels like it's on fire, but I'll live."

I motioned for her to head back towards the tram door with the others. I half expected my father to become enraged and yet here, in Mr. Eden's corporate office, he seemed much more timid. It was as if any and all aspects of strength in his character were being muted by these surroundings. He began to look frightened, and then he cried out in a pitiful plea that proved once and for all how far over the edge he'd gone.

"Adam! *Adam! They're taking him*! I don't know how to stop them, Adam." Then he became accusatory, almost as if he had to point the finger at someone else to take the blame for him. "It's *Jack*! *He's* the one that's doing it – and my mother. I've told you about her, Adam. Always meddling. *They're* the ones, Adam, not me. It's not me. No! No! No, I'm *strong*, Adam. Like you! Yes, I'm learning to be strong."

Jori called back from the far end of the room. "Jack, try the buttons on his desk. One of them has to activate this tram."

I moved toward the desk, and my father shook his head. "No! No! Jack, please. Adam will be so upset!"

I gritted my teeth and raised the metal bar. "Get out of my way." He began to back up.

"Adam! Adam, they're taking *Troy*! They're *stealing* him from you! You've got to do something or he'll be gone, Adam!"

I began frantically scoping out the buttons on his desk – there must have been twenty or thirty of them – but my head snapped up when I heard the ominous voice of Mr. Eden. I'd been so busy examining the buttons that I had missed the transformation this time. He was already wearing the hat and coat again.

"Step away from my desk, Jack." He reached for one of the buttons, and I slammed my weapon down on the desktop cracking the wood and missing his finger by less than a centimeter.

"I wouldn't do that if I were you." I was surprised at the steadiness of my own voice.

"All right." He took a step back. "But I don't think you should leave before I show you a little something I've been saving for a surprise." He reached into the pocket of his coat and pulled out a remote control. Before I could move to stop him, he pressed a button and the entire left wall of his office became transparent. We could see clearly into the room on the other side. It looked like some kind of research laboratory. There was evidence of technology everywhere. Gram, Jori, and I uttered a collective gasp. There. Just beyond the wall, lying on his side and facing us, was a battered figure. His eyes were closed. He was bound tightly in ropes and his mouth was sealed shut with duct tape. I could see that there were bruises all over his body, and his clothes were ripped and torn. He appeared to have been tortured and beaten. It was unclear whether he was alive.

Chapter Twenty-One

"*Troy!*" Gram was the first to speak. I looked back and saw her reach for Jori's arm to steady herself. Then, I looked down at the weapon in my hand and felt its weight. For the first time it felt good. I *wanted* to use it. With no warning, I whirled, swung toward him, and heard a "whiff" as the tire iron cleanly missed its target. He had anticipated me and sidestepped the intended blow with ease. Then, he looked at me smugly and laughed.

"Surely you don't think I can be overcome by such a primitive attempt as that, Jack. I would have thought better of you. Perhaps I should keep in mind that your emotions are likely running high right now. Your concentration is, no doubt, being affected."

"How do I know it's really Troy in that room?" The youth in the room hadn't moved. I didn't want to ask if he were alive because I didn't know if I could handle hearing the answer. "And if it *is* Troy, then . . . who's *he*?" I gestured toward the Troy I had wounded earlier.

"I'm your *brother*, Jack; what are you talking about? That double of me in the other room could be a hologram or a dummy. It could be anything. It isn't *real*. *I'm* real." He was staring deeply into my eyes the entire time he spoke, and I was searching for a trace of the truth from somewhere deep inside. Of course, a part of me wanted this boy to be my brother because it would mean that the battered figure inside the next room couldn't be the real Troy. And yet the fiery spirit that was so much a part of who Troy was seemed to be missing from the boy standing before me. I saw sincerity in his eyes; he really believed he was my brother, but *I* didn't believe it.

"This is really quite a *touching* family moment." Mr. Eden was smirking and laughing as he spoke to us.

"Yeah, well, we take every one we can get since the family seems to be disappearing at an alarming rate," I countered. "You wouldn't know anything about that, now would you?"

He glared at me and then fixed his gaze upon the boy who claimed to be my brother. "He doesn't believe you, Troy. He doesn't believe that you're his brother." Pause. "And he's correct. You *aren't*. You're *my* son. And you're *perfect.* You are *everything* a boy should be. Everything *my* boy should be."

"Why don't you tell him the whole truth," I said. "Tell him he's a machine, an android built to replace the real Troy. Why don't you tell him that? And while you're at it, you can explain why that chunk I took out of his leg really bled. How'd you create that little gimmick?" I was beginning to feel very bold. I had been right. This robot wasn't my brother. My father had been forced to admit it, or so I thought.

"You're a bright boy, Jack. Not as bright as *my* boy, of course. Don't worry, Troy, he . . ."

Before I even knew what was happening, a wave of anger engulfed me, and I took another swing at him with the rod. This time he was barely able to step back in time. The rod connected with the computer monitor on his desk and sent it crashing to the floor. *"Don't call him that!"* I raged. "He *isn't* Troy. Call him Benjamin or Daniel or Samuel. I don't care *what* you call him, but don't use my brother's name in reference to him again." The sound of my heartbeat began pounding in my ears, and I considered trying to take him out right then and there. I was ready to go after him with my bare hands if necessary. In a quick, smooth motion, he pulled the remote control from his jacket pocket again and pressed a button. The transparent wall became solid again.

"You don't make demands here, Jack. *I* am the owner of this corporation. I am the *ruler* of everything around me. I've been patient with you up to now, but that time has come to an end. Another outburst like that, and you'll never know what happened to your brother. Besides, you'll be interested to know that my son is *not* an android. He's nothing of the kind. He's *real!*" He walked toward us, came up behind his "son," and placed his hands on the boy's shoulders. "My son has been *genetically engineered!*"

"A clone?" I couldn't believe what I was hearing. "You *cloned* Troy? You can't just . . ."

He cut me off. *"I* can do anything. *Cloning* is such a primitive word for what I've done. I prefer the term *genetic engineering.*" He began to walk back around his desk as he talked. Clearly he was glorying in finally being able to explain the brilliance of his plans to me. I was keenly aware that, in the movies, the villain only explains the brilliance of his plans if he's about to get rid of the hero once and for all. I noticed Gram and Jori had moved farther away from us again. Gram's makeup bag was open, and they seemed to be scrutinizing the contents carefully. My father was ignoring them entirely – probably because he didn't think that there was anything any of us could do to him.

"It is true that I *borrowed* your brother in order to bring about the creation of my son."

"I like how you use the term 'borrowed.' That's pretty convenient. Let's see – you entered his room while he slept, knocked him out, and forcibly took him from his house without his knowledge. Then, you brought him – where? Here, maybe? So you could do . . . I don't know what to him! In a place where I used to live, called *reality*, I'd say that's a federal offense called *kidnapping*!"

He remained calm. "As I was saying, I did *borrow* Troy on several occasions. You see, he was just what I wanted – intelligent, handsome, strong, charming. There was just one problem – his *attitude* needed adjusting. He was so frustrating! Always challenging – never following the rules *exactly*. He wasn't obedient enough. So, I *borrowed* all of his best qualities and successfully corrected his deficiencies. *My* son is much more acquiescent than your brother. *My* son won't disappoint his father. The desire to please me has been instilled in him." He walked toward us again and spoke to his 'son.' "*You* are my most incredible success story. My greatest achievement. All of the others are androids – each one progressively better than the next. I've been working up to you!"

"So Gram was right. This whole village full of people – *none* of them are human." I couldn't keep the scorn from my voice.

"That's right," he said proudly. "I've been building Paradise for years! It's incredible! It's *perfection*. *Everyone* is happy here. We have no crime, no disease, no poverty. To live here is to experience a sense of peace, beauty, and contentment that can't be found in the outside world."

"But nobody *does* live here! That's just the point!" I argued. Was he so out of touch with reality that he didn't see it as a major problem that his village didn't have a very high percentage of living beings milling about?

"*I* live here. And now my son will live here with me. My wife is at home and the rest of my family will be with us soon."

"You may want to check on the grandmother," I said sarcastically. "I think she blew a fuse. Come to think of it, your wife wasn't looking too swell the last time I saw her either."

"A minor setback. They can be easily repaired."

"So why was Troy the only one cloned? Why not Mom, why not me, or Gram? Hey! Come to think of it, why not everyone? Why are there any androids at all?" I thought I knew the answer. I looked at his *son*. "Don't you wonder *why* you're the only one?"

The boy appeared genuinely overwhelmed by all of this information. I tried to imagine what it must be like to be him. He really had believed that I was his brother. I remembered his seeming reluctance to leave with us. Was that what my father had meant when he said he had instilled in the boy a desire not to disappoint his father? Still, it had appeared that he *might* leave with us. The boy looked at his "father," who was also *my* father. This was really getting wild.

"You *built* me?" he questioned.

"Created. I *created* you," came the gentle correction. "They're very different things." My father approached the clone and gingerly placed his hands on each side of the boy's face. "You are a *masterpiece*."

"But why only me?" The clone eyed his creator with genuine curiosity. I nodded at him inconspicuously – hoping to arouse his suspicions. *"Why aren't there more?"*

No reply. For a brief instant my father became vulnerable, and in that moment I pounced like a ravenous lion on a tender young lamb.

"Because he can't *control* a clone. Isn't that right? Isn't that what it's all about, power . . . and *control*?" I squared off against my father and my words went completely unchecked. "You can *control* an android. You can program it – *make* it do what you want. But with a clone, you can't guarantee the same level of obedience. I'm right, aren't I?" I turned back to the clone. *"That's* why you're the only one. He's going to have to spend a lot of time and energy trying to manipulate things so that you remain compliant. He couldn't manage the level of obedience he wants if he had more than one clone." As I began explaining everything to Troy's clone, the entire picture began to come more clearly into focus for me.

My implication – that something was beyond his control – enraged my father. "I can control *anything*! I control *everything* in Paradise! Everything! This is *my* domain. I have the power here!" He began shouting – trying to intimidate us all, but I hurled the truth back at him with just as much force.

"You brought us here to serve as models for androids so that when Troy's clone was ready, he'd already have a *perfect* family – one *entirely* under your control. TELL HIM THE TRUTH!" I could feel my fury melting into disgust for *Paradise* and everything it represented. I eyed the clone. "You were never going to know you were living in a village full of androids. He was going to copy us all and destroy us before they finished creating you, but the plan went awry – as plans for perfection so frequently do. We stuck around longer than he anticipated."

The clone's eyes grew wide. He looked to my father and then to me, causing me to wonder if I was forming an alliance. I continued the forward press. "Ask him about the boy in the other room – the one who looks like you. Ask if he's real. Ask if he was *hurt*. Ask *why* he was hurt. Ask if you can see him." By encouraging the clone to question his creator, I was hoping to raise even more doubts in his mind. Unfortunately, it seemed to have the opposite effect. He glanced at my father again and then toward the door through which he'd entered the room. It had no knob and had virtually disappeared into the wall. All at once, he began hobbling quickly towards it – dragging his injured leg just a bit. It opened immediately, and he slipped through the doorway just before it sealed itself again.

My father's face took on its most hideous *Mr. Eden* grin to date. "It's just as well that you upset him. I'd have difficulty convincing him that what I'm going to do to all of you is truly necessary if he were here to witness it. This way it will be much simpler." He began to slip his hand into his jacket pocket, but this time I was ready for him. I knew it was coming. The tire iron made heavy contact just as he pulled his hand from his pocket. He dropped the remote instantly – uttering a cry of pain that assured me that he would now view me as a serious adversary. As he bent down to retrieve his weapon, I came rushing at him hard – the iron held out in front of me with my hands gripping the two ends. I intended to hit him full force and knock him backwards to get him off balance. However, just as I expected him to rise up, he leapt toward my ankles – grabbing my legs and pulling us both toward the floor. My body thudded sickeningly against the marble tiles as he came down on top of me. Footsteps, I assumed Gram and Jori's, moved quickly in our direction, and I had only a moment to wonder why a *lady* cavalry was always coming to my rescue before my father grabbed the tire iron from my hands and pressed it to my throat.

"You and that *old* woman have caused me nothing but trouble from the beginning. Your father insisted you'd be no trouble – that he'd be able to control you. If I'd have followed my own plan, you'd have been out of the way immediately, and I'd never have had to dirty my hands with you. Still," he grinned as he pressed the iron deeper into my neck, "there is a certain satisfaction in doing the work myself."

The next thing I knew, there was blood splattering onto my face and my father's head whipped backwards so fast that I thought it was going to fly off his neck.

"*Whom* are you calling *old*?" Gram stood over him with a rolling pin in her hand. She'd obviously slammed him in the head with a good deal of force because an ample amount of blood was flowing down the right side of his face. I propped myself up and gave him a shove with my legs. He seemed disoriented, no big surprise, and fell over to my right side. Very quickly, though, he grabbed the remote, which was now within easy reach. He pointed it at her and pressed a button.

"Gram!" I screamed.

She slammed his wrist with the rolling pin, and the remote took flight again. He howled in protest.

"Stop playing with that thing. It won't do you one bit of good. I'm insulated!" she announced.

I looked down and saw that she was wearing rubber galoshes on her feet. Royal blue with magenta and white daisies on them. She showcased one for our inspection. "I did the flowers myself with tempera paint and stencils. What do you think?"

A fierce growl rose in his throat, and he prepared to lunge at her. WHAM! She plowed him in the head one more time, and he slumped to the floor. "It's not polite to growl at your mother. *Everyone* knows that," she said in a mocking robotic voice.

"Jack . . . Gram." We both turned at the sound of Jori's voice. Her tone was grave. Standing with her at the back part of the room was the clone. He was carrying Troy's limp body in his arms.

Chapter Twenty-Two

Gram and I moved quickly toward the sofa where they were laying Troy down. I noted the clone handling my brother gingerly and realized that it must have been painful for him to carry Troy's weight with his own leg having been so badly damaged by my earlier assault. No human being could have looked at my brother's body and not been moved with compassion. He didn't look like much of a wrestler at that moment. He looked like a little boy – the kind you see in photographs from books on child abuse. It was hard to find a spot on him that wasn't black and blue. Crusted blood covered his skin in several places, and there were rope burns around his wrists and ankles. Watching his chest rise and fall, I thanked God he was alive.

"Troy, darling." Tears streamed from Gram's eyes as she ever so delicately pressed her lips against his forehead. "Gram's here, honey. Jack and Jori are here, too. You're safe now. Troy? Sweetheart, can you hear me?" There was no response.

"Troy, come on, man." I tasted the salt of my own tears before I realized I was crying in front of Jori, but I didn't care. I grasped one of his hands in mine. "Troy, we came to get you out of here. It's all over. It's going to

be okay now. We're leaving this place forever."
Nothing. Was he in some kind of a coma? Had someone
beaten him so badly that he'd gone into shock?

"Let *me* try," Jori said. I was about to tell her that if
he wasn't going to respond to family, then he certainly
wasn't going to respond to a girl he'd only met once. But
when I looked at her face and saw the compassion
registering there, I decided to keep quiet. She moved to
the sofa and knelt on the rug beside it.

"Troy, it's Jori. Remember . . . from the gatehouse.
I've always heard that if people are breathing but not
conscious, they can still hear what others are saying to
them, so I just wanted to tell you that I told my sister,
Julie, about how good-looking you are . . . and, well, she
sort of has this *thing* for wrestlers. Anyway, she asked if
you were seeing anyone, and I told her . . ."

His eyes shot open. "No! You told her *no* right?" He
grinned ever so slightly and then groaned when he tried to
shift his body weight. "*Everyone* knows that I'm
currently a major bachelor stud, but when Julie and I
meet, I'll have to give up my wandering ways. What a
tragedy for the girls of this great nation. Maybe for girls
worldwide! What do you think, Gram? Do you think it
will be a tragedy for girls *worldwide* or just nationwide?"

She was dabbing at her eyes with a handkerchief as
she began to laugh. "Troy, darling, I've no doubt that
there will be an outpouring of grieving girls *worldwide*
when news that you are no longer eligible reaches their
ears."

He looked satisfied. "I thought so, too." Then he noticed the clone, and in typical, unflappable Troy fashion he said, "Hey, who's the good-lookin' kid?" The clone grinned and seemed to step into our circle a bit more – both physically and emotionally. He had taken a big risk by freeing Troy and bringing him to us.

"Oh, I'm nobody special. Just an up-and-coming teen idol!" The clone sparred with my brother quite naturally. Troy was, of course, impressed. He looked at me.

"Jack, this guy reminds me a lot of someone I know. I like his style. He's clever, outspoken, sociable yet sincere, self-confident but not arrogant, incredibly handsome and altogether a . . . ."

I glanced at Jori who was obviously amused. "You're the one who got him started. Can you *stop* him?"

"Am I detecting a note of sarcasm from my elder sibling, Grandmother?" We all began to laugh, and when the laughter subsided, the clone stepped forward and touched Troy's shoulder.

"I . . . I'm sorry about what he did to you. I didn't know. I didn't know anything about you. Really." I watched this young boy who in so many ways was like our own Troy and found myself deeply moved by his sincerity. It was as if he was maturing right before our eyes. Even Troy became serious for a moment. He regarded his double carefully and then reassured him of his innocence.

"Listen, buddy, a movie star face like that should never look so upset. Cheer up! I'll live. This wasn't your fault. I'm not always the most cooperative guy, so I took a little rough stuff. That's all."

I saw Troy looking at Gram, who was busy reorganizing the contents of her makeup bag. I knew that my father had tried to force him to reveal where she had been hiding. Troy had withstood the beatings to protect her, but he wasn't about to let her know it. I decided to keep his secret as well. "All right, gang, I say we get out of here and the sooner the better. Troy, can you walk?"

He sat up slowly. "Yeah. Just don't ask me to run any marathons, and I'll be fine."

Gram was standing with her makeup bag in hand. "Speaking of marathons," she winked at Troy, "we have to ditch this place so I can rest up and begin conditioning again. When Florence Petrillo gets a look at me during this year's Senior Sensation Marathon, she's going to be seeing me from *behind*!"

All at once, we heard a deep cough, the kind that makes it clear someone wants your attention. Jori grabbed my hand, but even before I turned around, I could tell by the terrified looks on their faces what had happened – we'd waited too long to leave. I turned to face him and was startled. Though he was still wearing the black trench coat and had replaced the hat which had fallen off when he tackled me, he looked different. The stream of dried blood on the right side of his face accounted for some of the difference, but not all of it. I really can't explain it. I'll never be able to, nor will any of the others, but it's something we all agree on. He

somehow seemed to have lost any physical resemblance
to my father whatsoever. He seemed larger and even
darker than before – more ominous, if that were truly
possible. At that moment, I felt that any good or rational
part of my father was gone – lost in a sea of insanity that
had finally engulfed him. Something settled, then, like a
boulder in the pit of my stomach. It was the certainty that
there was no part of him left that I would ever be able to
reach again; my father was gone.

As he stood behind his desk, the backdrop of the night
sky through the wall of windows directly behind him
seemed to enhance his shadowy appearance. He leveled
the remote at us and spoke with threatening intensity.

"You're all going to *die* now. All of you except my
boy. You've tried to poison him against me, but you
can't. And now, before you can do any more damage,
I'm going to rid my village of you. You're all *diseased*.
You're parasites. Imperfect. Flawed. You don't belong!
One at a time you're going to experience pain to a degree
that you have never conceived possible. I'm going to see
that each of you is *seared* alive – fried to ashes from the
inside out. *Electricity* is such a marvelous invention!
Now this can be quick, if there's no resistance. Or it can
be slow, and you can watch each other suffer."

Gram was trying to carefully open her makeup bag
without attracting any attention, but it didn't work. Mr.
Eden, that's how I thought of him at this point since my
father was most likely gone forever, pressed and released
the remote quickly, aiming it directly at Troy. A shot of

lightning seemed to appear out of nowhere and course through my brother's body. He screamed and fell to the ground.

"Drop the suitcase, old woman; drop it now!" He shouted at her in fury. "None of you move to help him, or you'll be next!" We froze in our tracks, and I heard the makeup bag drop to the floor. He aimed the remote at Troy again. "Now I'm going to rid the world of you and your rebellious attitude once and for all. You were a vital component in the creation of my son, but I've no need of you anymore."

Mr. Eden pressed the button with a look of devilish delight, but the clone had anticipated him and was quicker. Troy's double leaped into action and positioned his body so that my little brother, who was directly in the path of an intense electrical charge, was now shielded from harm. "NO!" The cry rose from deep inside of me, but I was far too late. The clone's body was incinerated, seared to ashes in seconds, right before my eyes. The smell of burnt flesh enveloped the room.

"NO!" He stepped out from behind his desk and fell to his knees as he began an impassioned plea. "Please, please . . . no! *Not him.* Not my *son.* He's the one I chose. He's *perfect!* We're alike. The *perfect* family. I had a plan for us! Everything would be *perfect!*"

Clearly he had never anticipated the possibility that Troy's double would sacrifice his life to protect someone else and, while he was clearly distraught over the loss of his son, he still clutched the remote in his hand. And that's where my attention was riveted. As he continued to sob and talk about his plans for the perfect world, I inched my way carefully toward him. I froze, though, when his head shot up abruptly. He looked me straight in the eye and charged me with a crime. "*You* caused all of this! It was *paradise* until you came."

I stared at him blankly. I couldn't have responded, even if I'd wanted to. I was stunned by how broken he appeared at that moment. It wasn't just that he *sounded* defeated – it was the way he looked – like I had single-handedly destroyed both his reality and his dreams. Which, come to think of it, I probably had.

He broke the silence with an anguished cry of rage. "*You shouldn't have come*! *None of you*!" His head shot wildly around the room as his eyes locked onto each one of us. "You don't belong here. You're not good enough! You have flaws! And now you've *infected* my village. You've brought all of your imperfections into a perfect society and LOOK!" He began shrieking like a madman and pointing all around the room – toward the broken computer monitor, the scarred top of his desk, and the pile of ashes that was once his son. "LOOK WHAT YOU'VE DONE TO MY WORLD! I can't *live* like this!" He turned the remote toward himself, but the screaming never let up for a moment. "No man could! I can't be expected to survive in these conditions! It's *insanity*! INSANITY – that's what it is!"

"*Dad*."

The title was delivered softly, carefully. It took a minute for me to realize that it came from me. He looked so pitiful at that point – like a child who was lost in a crowd – that I just couldn't help myself. And then he looked at me. We studied each other for a while. I don't know what he was thinking in those few moments of silence, but I was thinking about something my English teacher, Mrs. Schott, had told us earlier in the year. We were discussing multiple themes in a novel we'd been reading about a Utopian society, and she reminded us that somewhere, somehow, some*one* always pays the price for perfection. She said it's a much higher price than most people realize.

And that's when he pressed the button. Right in the middle of my flashback to Honors English he made his decision. He could not exist in the real world – the world he was born into – because society was, by his standards, defective. And because of us, his fantasy was crumbling. Because of us, he had realized that perfection would remain elusive – even on *this side of Paradise*. The discharge of electricity sent his body into a dramatic series of seizures, probably because the remote was so close to him when he activated it. He shrieked in excruciating pain, and I leapt backwards just in time to see his body somehow detonate from the inside out. I've often wondered whether it was my father or Mr. Eden who made the decision to end his life. I don't know if I'll ever know for sure. But one thing I do know is that Mrs.

Schott was right. The price for perfection *is* much higher than most people realize.

We discovered, much later, that he took them all with him. Every android he'd created, including Mr. Simpson, was reduced to an unrecognizable pile of rubble through some kind of bizarre chain reaction that must have occurred the moment he ceased to exist. Gram had several private investigators look into the fate of the *real* Mr. Simpson, but none of them turned up anything. It took a while for her to adjust to the idea that her good friend could be buried in an unmarked grave somewhere. The probability of his death gave her more than a few sleepless nights, but she adjusted to the loss in time.

Troy did not fair as well. The news of Mom's death devastated him to the point that he nearly shut down on us completely. He had no appetite, and he rarely left the house. He dropped out of everything at school, including wrestling. He wouldn't even return phone calls from *cheerleaders*. When Gram or I tried to get him to talk about what was wrong, he'd make some clever comeback to avoid really addressing the issue. Luckily, Gram took note of his downward spiral and had all three of us seeing a grief counselor in no time – some weird guy who wore tye-dye suits and had a juke box in his office that played country music. She'd met him at a seminar she'd attended in the Rockies last year called *A New You for the New Millennium*. He was quirky to say the least, but that worked to our benefit because none of Troy's shenanigans exasperated him. It took a few months, but in the end, he helped each of us begin the grieving process in our own way, and our work with him was a strong reminder to me that I shouldn't judge on first impressions. Most importantly, he helped Troy find his way out of a depression that was crippling him, and for that Gram and I will always be grateful.

I pulled Gram's little red sports car into Jori's driveway at quarter to eleven. Despite the fact that it was a beautiful, relaxing morning, Troy was fidgeting nervously in the passenger's seat and drumming his fingers on the armrest. I was watching him and enjoying myself immensely. *Mr. Cool* was a nervous wreck about meeting Jori's sister, Julie.

"What do you think I should say for an opener, Jack? You got any ideas?" His eyes were darting nervously between their front door and me.

"How should *I* know? What's the matter *Dr. Love*? Don't tell me you've lost your touch!" I said sarcastically.

"Stop it, Jack. This girl's going to be different, and you know it. She's Jori's sister!"

"So?" I didn't see his point.

"*So* there's a very good chance that she won't go for any of my cheesy pick-up lines!" His state of panic was intensifying the more he talked. I was loving every minute of this.

"So don't use any of them. Then you don't have to worry about them blowing up in your face." I grinned. I could predict his frustrated reply even before I heard it.

"Jack, that's all I *have*! They always worked until Jori came along."

"Not on the girls in Paradise," I corrected him.

"They don't count. They weren't real girls. Besides, if I embarrass myself in front of her before we even leave for the airport, the whole day will be a bust!" A pause. I said nothing. Let him sweat.

Finally he put forth a pathetic and impassioned plea. "I'm going to sit here like a complete doofus if you don't help me! Come on, Jack, please!"

At precisely that moment, Jori and Julie stepped out onto the porch of their neatly trimmed two-story house. "Well, Mr. Doofus, I'd love to help you out, but – you're out of time!" I motioned toward the house with my head, and he followed my gaze. They were almost to the car. We both got out, and I raced around to greet Jori while he stood by the passenger's door like a statue. The girls grinned at us and held up matching bags that they were carrying. My face broke into a wide smile.

"A little big for a *purse* – don't you think?" I questioned her as I made a move to look inside the bag.

She snatched it back. "Ah, ah, ah! You stay out of there, Jack Barrett!"

Julie, who was even more stunning in person than in the picture Jori had shown me, smiled warmly at Troy, and I thought he was going to pass out. "Your grandmother sent them to us," she explained. "What a nice lady! And they have the most *interesting* things inside of them!"

"Oh."

I had to bite my tongue to keep from laughing out loud. *Oh*. That's all he could say to her! This was indeed a rich moment in my life. An awkward pause followed as we waited for Troy to say something more to Julie, but he remained silent and stared at the ground as though he had just discovered that he had feet. Too bad I didn't have a video camera. My brother was finally tongue-tied around a girl. I wondered if Julie was the outgoing type or more of the shy, you-can-lead-the-conversation-and-make-all-of-the-decisions type. I was praying for the latter so that he would *have* to talk to her.

"Troy, maybe you should let Julie in the car," I suggested in a bit of a condescending tone. Now he couldn't say that I hadn't helped him out. The sound of my voice seemed to snap him back to attention. He opened the door and pulled the passenger's seat forward to allow her to climb into the back. Julie eyed him and smiled as she began to step into the car. Then, she stopped and backed out before she was even halfway in. She surveyed him again. "Has anyone ever told you that you're *terribly* good-looking?"

My jaw dropped so fast it's a wonder that I didn't dislocate it. Troy, on the other hand, responded like a toy that had just come to life.

"As a matter of fact," he took her hand and helped her into the car, "just the other day a bunch of girls were talking about how much I have in common with those guys in those teen pin-up magazines. Well, I told them I *do* work out and all, but I don't know if I'm as . . . "

I let the seat fall back into position as he climbed in after Julie, and Jori took her place up front. As the engine fired up and I sped off toward Davenport Community Airport, I looked at Jori and chuckled. "The kid just can't lose." We held hands, and I listened to her singing softly to tunes on the radio as I raced down the highway toward our destination. From what I could hear of the backseat conversation, Troy was gearing up to make Julie the new president of his fan club, and from the sound of things, she was ready to accept the nomination. So once again my grandmother had been right. She had said, soon after leaving Paradise, that life would go on.

"Things will get better," she told us. "My attorneys and Judge Dreyer are working with the county court system, and I think those judges have been convinced that the county should assume responsibility for the village at this point. Thankfully, they aren't asking a lot of questions. Greg Dreyer has a way with those county judges, and *I* have a way with Greg Dreyer," she said running her fingers nonchalantly through her hair. "So there you have it." She looked directly into our eyes, reached for both Troy's hand and mine, and placed them gently between hers as she spoke. "Paradise will fade from our memories over time, but we'll never completely forget it. And you know something, boys? I'm not sure we ever should."

Parking at our little community airport on a Sunday was a "no-brainer" and as I pulled into a space, I began wondering what in the world my grandmother had in store for us. When she had first asked us to meet her here, I assumed she had hired a pilot to take us flying; however, when I questioned her further, she was so tight-lipped that I'd become certain it wasn't anything that simple.

"Hey, everyone! You're right on time!" She stepped out from behind the rear area of one of the planes that we had just walked past.

"Gram? What were you doing back there?"

"Just getting a few pointers from Duke. Say hello to the kids, Duke!" She barked at a pair of legs that were all we could see of "Duke."

"Hello, kids!" responded a muffled voice which was followed by a good deal of banging and clanging.

Gram dusted herself off and embraced each of us in turn. She was wearing a black form-fitting jumpsuit with matching gloves and a pair of fancy leather tie-up boots. She had some kind of sporty looking goggles on her head and what looked like a strangely-shaped pillow strapped behind her petite frame.

"Gram, what's that thing on your back?" I questioned as she began leading us toward a little office building. I could see her makeup bag on a bench out front.

"Oh, this?" she answered casually. "Just a little parachute."

"A PARACHUTE! Gram! What are you thinking? You *can't* be serious. *Skydiving!* You could . . ."

"Now Jack Edward Barrett you listen to me, and you listen well. I've been discussing this with Duke, he's the pilot, for over a week, and I'm bound and determined to do it. Besides, Florence Petrillo went snorkeling off the Great Barrier Reef last month with her granddaughter, and that's all I've heard about for days. She even has the pictures to prove it."

"Gram you have to stop competing with Mrs. Petrillo all the time. Just because she went snorkeling with her granddaughter doesn't mean that you have to . . ."

A heavy hand clapped me on the shoulder. "You ready, young fella?"

"Yes, Duke. He's ready," Gram said.

"Huh? Ready for what?"

"Why, the *big* jump! Today's the day. Your grandmother's told me all about how you've been lookin' forward to this." He began moving my arms through the loops that would hold the parachute to my back. "I must say, though, you're lookin' kinda peaked right now. You feelin' okay?"

"He's fine, Duke. Don't worry about him." Gram leaned over and punched my arm playfully. "Just wait until Florence sees *our* picture!"

Gram and the girls walked the rest of the way over to the bench to pick up her makeup bag while Troy, who had been lying on the ground convulsing in gales of laughter, finally got up and came over to me.

"Did you know about this?" I eyed him warily.

"No idea – Scout's honor."

"You were kicked out of the Scouts, Troy."

"*Their* loss. Jack, I'm telling you the truth. I had no idea why we were coming here today. Don't worry. It can't be that bad. People do it all the time."

"That's right!" said Duke. He had gone back to the plane and had just returned with another chute. He gave Troy's shoulders a firm grip from behind and rocked him forward a bit in a friendly gesture. "I've never seen two boys so devoted to their grandmother. And you . . ." He turned Troy around to face him just as the girls rejoined us. "You are *really* something, little buddy. Taking photographs while you're skydiving is tricky business. You'll need to handle the equipment very carefully, you know what I mean?"

I watched as realization dawned in Troy's eyes. He looked at Duke in a panic. "Who? Me! ME! *I'm* the photographer?"

I saw Gram quietly removing a rose from her makeup bag as she tracked the flow of conversation between Troy and the pilot. Duke began strapping a parachute onto Troy and explaining that the way it opened would be a bit *different*. Also, Troy would have to jump first because he'd need to be below Gram and me in order to get the best shots.

"Can't this be done from the ground?" Troy pleaded.

"What a kidder he is, Duke. I love that about him!" Gram elbowed Troy and said quietly, "Sweetheart, you don't want a man named *Duke* to think you're a big wuss do you?   Now stop it, or you'll embarrass your grandmother. Besides, it can't be that complicated. If worse comes to worst, you can figure it out on the way down." She looked at the rest of us and said in a conspiratorial tone, "According to Duke, it takes a lot longer to *hit* the ground than most people think."

She didn't wait for a response but called on us to follow her to the plane while Duke headed back to activate his flight plan. Within moments the five of us were walking arm in arm while the warm breeze danced all around us. Gram, who was at one end of the line, lifted her rose and blew on it softly. We all watched as one petal was released and began its waltz with the wind. In that moment, I looked at each of them in turn and grinned, "Now *this*," I told them, "is *my* idea of paradise!"

EPILOGUE

He leaned back in his chair and rested his feet on the wide desk in front of him. It had been a long frustrating day filled with too many decisions. He'd had to leave the building and interact with so many people out in the world today. Those people annoyed him. They were inept, foolish, incompetent . . . *weak*. Here, he was protected from them. The intercom on his desk beeped.

"Yes, Constance?"

"Before I leave for the evening, Sir, is there anything else that I can do for you?"

"No, no. Constance, everything's fine. Just fine." Pause. "Constance?"

"Yes, Sir?"

"Why did you ask me if there was anything else you could do for me before you left for the day?"

"Why *all* good employees ask their bosses that question at the end of the day, Sir. *Everyone knows that.*"

He smiled. He knew what her response would be, but he still took great satisfaction in hearing her say it. He picked up the blueprints for the buildings that would occupy the third city block. Things were moving along quite nicely. A voice mail message earlier in the day had notified him that the sign would be delivered tomorrow.

He would take great pains to be certain that *this* sign was installed correctly. Instantly, his head began to throb – just as it did each time he thought about the error that had been made with the sign for the original village. Some inept workman had installed it *outside* of the entrance gate. Of course, it had then been necessary to allow the sign to decay because it was not located within the village boundaries. This time, though, it would be different. He would make certain of that. There would be no mistakes this time. None. Then, he smiled with smug satisfaction and reminded himself that in another six months the entire downtown would be operational.

At first, it had been difficult working outside the United States. He disliked the way real estate was transacted in foreign countries. Buying up enough land was always the first and most difficult step. Then, came coordinating the schedules of the builders and their contractors which consistently tested his tolerance level for idiots and fools. They were slow, unreliable, and inefficient. Still, he always needed them for a while – at least until he learned enough about the laws and building codes in an unfamiliar country to navigate around potential difficulties. Eventually though, generally as quickly as possible, he saw to it that they were all *replaced*.

He looked at the clock – 5:46 P.M. He would need to leave now in order to arrive home promptly at 6:00 P.M. for dinner. They would all be waiting for him. He walked to the closet, opened the door, and removed his hat and coat. Then he traced the familiar path to the elevators. Most of the staff had gone home for the day at 5:00 P.M., but he noted lights on in a few inner offices where some dutiful employees were no doubt catching up on excess paperwork.

He boarded the elevator and carefully regarded his watch as the doors closed. The ride down to the bottom floor was uneventful. At this time of day Cora knew where he was going, and the two of them did not engage in conversation. His routine was simply to enter the elevator and fixate on his watch until the doors sealed shut. Hers was to dutifully select the ground floor button and serve as his silent companion during the descent. Only when he departed would she acknowledge him. That is how he wanted it, and she responded accordingly.

The doors opened, and he stepped from the elevator.

"Good night, Mr. Eden," she said as the doors began to close once more.

He ignored her as he always did. He was preoccupied with his watch for a moment, but at last an enormous grin revealed his delight. "Right on time," he observed with satisfaction. "Absolutely *perfect!*"

Photograph by Bob Luse

Steven L. Layne serves as director of the Master of Education in Literacy program at Judson University in Elgin, Illinois, where he teaches courses in reading methodology as well as in children's and adolescent literature. Dr. Layne is a respected literacy consultant, motivational keynote speaker, and featured author both in and outside of the United States.

Dr. Layne has been honored with numerous awards for his work as an educator. In 2001, he received one of the Milken Family Foundation's Educaton Awards for excellence in teaching. He was also named to the 2001 All-USA Teacher Team by *USA Today* and was chosen as the Edwin A. Hoey Award winner for Outstanding Middle School Educator by the National Council of Teachers of English in 2001. He was the 2000 ICARE for Reading Award winner and the 1999 Junior High Reading Educator of the Year.

Steven L. Layne is the author of several other books published by Pelican:

The Teachers' Night Before Christmas, an International Reading Association/Children's Book Council Children's Choices selection

My Brother Dan's Delicious, an International Reading Association/Children's Book Council Children's Choices selection

Over Land and Sea: A Story of International Adoption, one of *Learnin*g magazine's Books for Special Kids for Back-to-School

- *Paradise Lost*
- *Mergers*
- *Verses for Dad's Heart*
- *Verses for Mom's Heart*
- *The Principal's Night Before Christmas*
- *Preacher's Night Before Christmas*
- *Teachers' Night Before Halloween*
- *Thomas's Sheep and the Spectacular Science Project*
- *Thomas's Sheep and the Great Geography Test*
- *Love the Baby*
- *Stay with Sister*
- *Share with Brother*
- *My Brother Dan's Delicious / Love the Baby CD*
- *This Side of Paradise CD*